GW00725462

DIABOLICAL LIBERTY

G. LLEWELLYN BARKER

NEW HAVEN PUBLISHING LTD UK

First Edition
Published 2016
NEW HAVEN PUBLISHING LTD
www.newhavenpublishingltd.com
newhavenpublishing@gmail.com

Cover design©Jenna Bushell

newhaven
publishing
Copyright © 2016 G. Llewellyn Barker
All rights reserved
ISBN:
ISBN: 978-1-910705-60-5

To Evelyn and Geo

Acknowledgements

Thanks to Teddie Dahlin, JEB

and Street Sounds magazine.

Book One: Road To Hell

7   *Prologue*
7   *The Office*
10 *Just Like Eddie*
14 *Ready To Ruck*
22 *Enter Sandman*
23 *I Don't Like Mondays*
25 *Commuter In A Stupor*
28 *The Dark Lantern*
35 *Wednesday's Child*
39 *Fire, I'll Take You To Burn*
47 *Waterloo Sunset*
52 *Police Car*
59 *Thomas Scrimshaw is In A Cell, OK*
61 *ACAB: All Coppers Are...*
62 *The Trial*

Book Two: Roads To Nowhere

77   *Prologue II*
78 *Philosophy? Don't Get Me Sartre'd*
103 *Welcome To The House Of Fun*
115 *Dizzy Detour*
127 *Roads To Nowhere - one: The Gangs of New Cross*
132 *Roads To Nowhere - two: Trouble Is Coming, Temptation*
147 *Picture This*

Book Three: Roads To Freedom

152 *Rock World*
161 *Thomas Sees All*
165 *Valhalla, I Am Coming*
170 *Crazy Train*
173 *Hammer Of The Gods*
176 *I Am The Resurrection*
181 *Some Might Say; An Epilogue*
183 *Appendix*

Diabolical Liberty

Book One: The Road to Hell

Prologue

Day 13 It looked like an open and shut case. A fresh corpse on the ground, a reputable man of God as the only eye witness and a clearly identified suspect who just happened to be a) an escaped prisoner, recently convicted of arson, b) a notorious trouble-maker and c) a known anarchist.

He also happened to be me.

Tomorrow's newspapers would have a field day. Twitter already had. The trouble was I was I hadn't done it. I hadn't done anything! Granted I was on the run from the police, but the only thing that I'd ever set alight was a Christmas pudding; and the closest I'd ever got to anarchy was my old man's punk rock collection.

I was as innocent as Snow White cuddling a new-born lamb at an infant school fete. All of the evidence against me was either circumstantial or maliciously invented for reasons I cannot begin to fathom. Nothing makes sense and it hasn't done for quite a time. To make things worse, my only hope appears to lie with an oddball private dick.

I suppose I'd better start at the beginning.

The Office

Day One. Brian Clarkson, the balding head of my department, called me in for my first appraisal. My watch was slightly faster than his clock. Mine said 16:47. Everything about Clarkson's office screamed 1958. It reeked of furniture polish and Middle England, of hanging on in quiet desperation until you drew your last pitiful breath or your even more pitiful pension. There were probably morgues in Helmand Province that felt more welcoming.

Clarkson himself looked like a depressed walrus. "Well, sit down, lad," he said impatiently. He pressed the intercom with a podgy finger and summoned my supervisor, Miss Simms, aka "the Crimplene Dragon". Twenty-seven years in London hadn't erased the Grangetown from his diction. Ignoring me, he studied the open folder on his desk. How long would this shit take? I'd been working for the Authority ever since I left school. There wasn't a day when I didn't miss double maths.

The door opened. Enter The Dragon. Clarkson turned his gimlet eyes to me. "Now then," he said, peering over the top of his glasses, "Three months you've been 'ere, young Scrimshaw, but I'm not convinced your attitude or your behaviour are entirely appropriate."

My face didn't fall; it plummeted. Where was this coming from?

"My behaviour? Have I done something wrong, sir?"

"Miss Simms here tells me that you've been rolling in from lunch smelling of alcohol."

"Maybe once," I replied truthfully. "But it was a birthday drink and I'd only had a shandy."

"Mr. Dugash says you have a problem with time-keeping."

Dugash! The dead-eyed head of security. "I, er..."

Clarkson produced a memo, and began to read it. "Friday September 13th, you arrived back from lunch one minute and 45 seconds late...September 20th, four minutes late, September 27th, three minutes 17 seconds..."

I groaned inwardly. The barrel containing my prospects was rapidly approaching Victoria Falls.

"You've been late back to work seven times."

"By a minute or two, sir, that main road is a devil to cross."

"But only on a Friday, eh boy?"

"Pub!" snorted Miss Simms.

The weekly trip to Forbidden Planet actually.

I felt my face turn red as I scrambled for words. "I, I..."

"I should remind you that you are seventeen, and the legal age for drinking is eighteen."

"Sir."

"And you day-dream, boy, isn't that right?"

Where was this going? I felt like I'd wandered into a mine-field, wearing blinkers, on a really windy day.

"He's very dreamy," said Miss Simms without looking up from her nails. "He's in another world, dreaming his life away, killing time."

"But he does the job?"

"Oh yes, he does what he's told quite efficiently."

Clarkson shook his big, round bowling ball of a head. "Listen Thomas, I'm not going to let you go at this stage. You do what you're asked and that may be enough for some employers, but to get on here you need to show initiative, lad. We need dynamic, self-starting folk. I think your social life may become a problem; you seem to spend an inordinate amount of time away from your desk in the afternoons. Mr. Dugash has provided information on that too."

He brandished another print-out. I'd started to feel like a lamppost outside a kennel club.

"I don't think..." I began to say.

"No don't think, just listen. You're on my time here, boy, and I don't like to see it wasted. You've been here three months and you've not set the world alight. I'm going to extend your probation for three more months to give you the opportunity to knuckle down and show me what you're made of. It's 2014, not the 1970s and slacking just will not do. That's it, Scrimshaw. You can go now. But remember, I want to see energy. I want burning ambition. Got that?"

"Yes Mr. Clarkson."

"Good, now get on with you."

I got up and flashed an angry finger at the sanctimonious buffoon ...in my mind. In reality I shuffled out, collected my army surplus great-coat and bag from my desk, and walked down to the foyer. Dugash the sadist was loitering in the shadows, skinny, bald and stone-faced. The fifty-first shade of grey. He looked like Munch's Scream in a suit.

Outside it had started to snow. I turned up my coat collar and trudged to the train station. There was an old vagrant, an Asian or Middle Eastern guy, sitting in an alley outside Waterloo East.

"Here you go mate," I said, slinging a £5 note into his hat. "Merry Christmas, grandad...even if you, uh, don't celebrate it."

School had taught us to be culturally sensitive.

"God bless you, boy," the tramp muttered.

"Someone better had."

"Someone may well."

As I walked away a pleasant wave of tingling warmth spread right through me. It only lasted four or five seconds and I was too wrapped up in self-pity to pay it any heed. Head down, I carried on walking. I would only have spent the money on *Vive Le Rock* or something similar. I had to do something with my life. I was in a rut and I had to get out of it. I...

Behind me he heard a gruff voice growl at the vagrant: "Gertcha, get a job, you old bastard."

Commuters. So full of Christmas spirit.

Just Like Eddie

I didn't remember getting home at all, but here I was in my bedroom listening to Rammstein. It was a small box room, just ten feet by eight, but every spare inch of the walls was covered with pictures and newspaper cuttings. Salvador Dali competed with rock posters, Tolkien imagery, Marvel superheroes, the wolves, trolls and gods of Viking mythology, and pictures of kestrels, swallows and chaffinches which nested next to a more recent bird fixation – half-naked ones cut carefully from Loaded Magazine. I also had an autographed picture of Anna Paquin – Sookie from True Blood – an Ally McBeal promotional snap of Calista Flockhart from a boot sale, a shot of the late trade union leader Bob Crow to wind up my fuckwitted step-father, and rare complimentary headlines about Charlton Athletic Football Club (ditto). My bookshelves were heaving with paperbacks, astronomy hardbacks, grotesque skulls and comedy DVDs. Under the bed, were a mess of graphic novels and a well-thumbed collection of poorly-written men's mags that I'd inherited from a cousin. Unusual woman. I had a BOSE sound system, my own TV, and a second-hand iPad with a screensaver of Eddie from Iron Maiden.

Downstairs my mum and step-dad had just started their traditional evening row. I turned up the music to drown out their bickering. Was all adult life like this? I had trouble remembering a time when they didn't argue. There had been a brief few months after Mum had remarried when she had seemed happy with horrible Frank Pearce, but I suspected she'd been kidding herself. They'd had a fling when she was married to my real father. Dad was a chippie; he worked long hours to pay the mortgage and Mum, feeling neglected, had been easy prey. Or at least that was my charitable take on it. But what on earth had made her chose Frank over Dad? They had nothing at all in common. She was soft, dreamy and imaginative. He was a lazy slob who thought with his fists. Manky Frankie; Frank The Plank I'd like to spank. Not that fighting was my thing, you understand.

I disliked everything about the man, from his Palace tattoo to his big crimson face: the smell of his breath, the veins on his nose, the fridge packed with his crap supermarket own brand lager, the ever-expanding wodge of flab over his belt. I hated the way he ate, the way he voted, the way he rolled home from his local, which in my mind was called the Fuehrer & Firkin, reeking of cheap bitter, self-pity and belligerence.

To the best of my knowledge Frank had never hit Mum. If he ever did, I hoped I'd be man enough to stand up to the creep.

Downstairs a plate smashed. What was it about this time? The slightest thing set them off; they bickered from morning till night, on and bloody on. It was like living with Itchy and Scratchy.

Whatsapp buzzed. It was Mark Gladberry, my oldest mate.

'Yo, Tom, howdit go m8? U gt raise?'

'Nah. Zilch. Clarkson jst chewed me out LOL.'

'WTF. Y?'

'Sed I lack burning ambition.'

'WTF?'

'I shda torched the fat toad.'

'ROFL. U out 2nite?'

'Prbly not. 2moro, k?'

Downstairs the argument had escalated. Another plate smashed. 'Gotta go,' I typed.

'L8ers.'

I ejected the Germans and flicked through my CDs for something livelier to reflect his mood. Yeah, Agnostic Front. That would do the trick. Most of my mates were i-Tunes all the way, but I preferred to have something physical. It seemed... more real.

Now I was earning there was no reason not to leave home; no reason not to take that first small inevitable step into the great karmic blizzard of grown-up life. No reason of course except fear.

I scanned the back of the case looking for Gotta Go then remembered that it was on a different album.

"How about Linkin Park?" said a voice in a slurred Birmingham accent.

"Great idea", I said. "Wha...?"

I span around. There was no one else in the room.

"Crawling is such a great song, man."

The voice was coming from the poster of Ozzy Osbourne on my wall. I stared at it in disbelief.

"No dude, go for Manic Depression." That was Kurt Cobain.

"Rage Against The Machine, por favor comrade." chipped in Che Guevara.

I felt dizzy.

The pictures and posters on my bedroom walls were coming alive.

Had Frank been spiking my tea? Or was I just going nuts?

"Some people say I'm bonkers, but I just think I'm free," opined Dizzee Rascal. "Man I'm just living my life, there's nothin' crazy about me."

Maybe it was one of those hidden camera TV shows like Punk'd. I looked around for a craftily concealed lens but was immediately distracted. Ozzy Osbourne's face on the Ozzfest bill had become three-dimensional. It had also started to glow and pulsate.

A cold sweat broke out on my temples. I felt hot, baffled, scared. I wanted to move, but my legs wouldn't respond. My stomach went in to a spasm, my balls tightened and my entire body started to tingle. I tried to shout but no words came out. I felt pressure on the top of my head followed by intense pain. My hands shot up. I could feel my head physically stretching. It was agonising, as if someone was bombarding my skull, inside and outside, with innumerable red-hot needles; and this burning, searing, scorching sensation was gnawing through me, seeping through my brain and down my spinal column.

I had never experienced pain like it. Every part of my head ached, my ears, nose, mouth, teeth, tongue. It was torment. Excruciating. I felt like my brain was going up in flames. Then my body started to move...

Someone or something, some weird unseen force, was sucking me head-first towards the wall.

That was when I wet myself.

In the distance I heard a woman shout. Not Mum. It sounded like "Help me, Tommy." It was dark but there were small fiery pits all around me and heard my name again.

"THOMAS!"

That was Mum that time, but where was she? More to the point, where was I? I was upright but my body was doing a strange dance. My legs were stretched akimbo and flames scorched my feet. I moved frantically, trying to find safer ground as I took in the wild scenes all around me. Everywhere I looked, people writhing and twisting besides blazing fires. I heard the first woman shout "Tommy, help." Where was she? Where was I? The scene was as familiar as it was hellish, yet I couldn't quite place it. I couldn't concentrate on anything because I couldn't stop dancing. My limbs were completely beyond my control.

"Thomas!"

Dad always called me Tommy. To everyone else I was Tom, although I had suffered a month of being 'Harry' to my schoolmates when JK Rowling-In-It was all the rage. Of course I'd had my hair cropped immediately.

My feet were stinging with pain. My wrists were sore. There were strings tied to them and to my ankles too. I followed them upwards. They were attached to a giant red hand belonging to an enormous leering Lucifer. I screamed like a girl and tried to turn and run but the strings stopped me. Shivering with fear, I turned back to look at Beelzebub, the very face of evil. There was something else up there too though. Towering above Satan was an even larger figure – Iron Maiden's monstrous mascot Eddie, who appeared to be operating Old Nick with strings just as the devil was working me.

That's when I realised why everything looked so familiar. I was inside the Iron Maiden poster that hung opposite my bed, next to Tyra Banks and a Helen Flanagan topless shot I'd torn out from a copy of the *Daily Star* that I'd found on an 89 bus. I was IN the Number Of The Beast poster. In fact, if I squinted through the smoke and flames, I could just about make out my gothic-black duvet cover. But how....? What the devil was going on?

"Thomas!"

The bedroom door burst open and Mum walked in just as I landed in a heap on the floor. It was like her presence had broken the spell. Mum was still in auto-rant mode. "Will you tell Frank...," she said before noticing me at her feet. "Frank! Get up here," she shouted. "I think he's having a fit."

If she had looked a bit closer, Mum would have noticed that my clothes were singed and my hair was smouldering.

Ready To Ruck

Day Two. I decided against telling my friends about my strange bedroom experience. It seemed too nuts, even for me. Someone must have spiked my drink. Possibly Phyllis Simms. I momentarily imagined her coming at me naked except for a coquettish grin and nearly gagged on my bacon roll, Ed Miliband style.

"You okay there Tommy?" asked Kez.

"He's only choking," grinned Matt, giving my back a hefty slap.

"That's the trouble with bacon, it makes your eyes go streaky," cut in Mark.

"If he doesn't want it, I'll have it," said Matt. "I love bacon so much when I eat it I get a lard-on."

"Inappropriate," Kez tutted, adding "From groan to gross in five seconds, that's got to be a record even for you two dorks."

Every other Saturday the four of us would meet in Gambadella's, an old-fashioned cafe at the Blackheath Royal Standard, before going to watch Charlton at The Valley. In the evening we'd normally mooch on to a punk and indie disco in the local liberal club.

I'd known Mark since primary school; we'd gone to our first gigs and our first football matches without adults together. We'd even written our first song together, me on guitar and him on the kazoo. (It was called The Laughing Weasel and it was crap.) Matt was a year older and worked in the post room at my office; and Kez – Keziah Lillian Smith – was a doctor's daughter from Bromley who we'd chummed up with at Quasar, the laser gun stadium game. We called her Lucky Lil because she had never been known to leave a fruit machine out of pocket.

Kez was a naturally pretty brunette with high cheekbones and oriental eyes – her mother was Vietnamese. Yet she chose to sabotage her looks by wearing no make-up and tying her hair back under a baseball cap. To us, she was just one of the lads; the one who thrashed us at pool, played the best poker and could talk us under the table.

It was Kez who changed the natural rhythm of our Saturday by saying that a local punk band called the Toerags were playing that night at a student union bar in SE1. Matt had been to school with Priyan, the guitarist, and a quick mobile phone call got us on the guest-list. So at 6.30pm we were spilling out at Waterloo East station.

As we walked past the neighbouring alley I heard a whimper of pain. An elderly vagrant was being roughed up by three burly meat-heads in leather jackets who appeared to think they were auditioning for a Clockwork Orange re-make.

"Hey, pack that in," I yelled.

"Make us, ya mouthy cunt," the biggest yob sneered.

Mark, a front row rugby prop, shot Matt, a decent amateur boxer, a look that said "Let's have it." They piled in to two of the attackers who swiftly retreated. I told Kez to stand back and squared up to the remaining bully. That's when the first small waves of doubt splashed through my mind followed immediately by a tsunami of fear. The yob looked two years older than me, was four inches taller and three stone heavier. His face was sullen and defiant, his ape-like shoulders were stooped and the two fat arms that had been swinging menacingly by his sides like legs of tattooed mutton opened up in the unmistakable 'come-on-then' gesture common to angry football hooligans and silverback gorillas everywhere.

I gulped, but there was no backing down. I ran at him and landed a haymaker on his chin. It was the best punch I had ever thrown and it had absolutely no effect. A moment later I was on the floor under a torrent of blows. I saw a boot raised above my head, curled into a protective ball and prepared for pain that never came. Instead I heard the sound of breaking wood, as Kez smashed the old tramp's cane over my opponent's shaven skull. I looked up and saw that the bully-boy's head was bleeding nicely. Unfortunately he was still standing.

As he began lurching towards Kez, she swerved like Catwoman and wacked him again. I was attempting to get up just as Mark and Matt ran back.

"Come on!" shouted Mark.

The big lug hesitated. "I'll have you, ya stinkin' Paki lovers," he said, taking a step backwards. "I'm Joey Bishop. Remember that name cos you're gonna pay for this."

"Yeah, yeah, on yer bike, caveman," said Kez.

Bishop jabbed a finger at me. "I'll have you and yer trappy bird," he snarled. He backed out of the alley to laughs of derision.

Kez ran over to me, helping him to my feet.

"You OK, Rambo?" she asked.

"Yes thanks, trappy bird."

We laughed. "Thanks again, son," said the vagrant in a voice that was as rich and heavy as French onion soup. He sounded like Patrick Stewart with extra bass.

I looked at him properly for the first time and realised that he was the old dosser from outside my office. Up close he wasn't as ancient as he'd first appeared; early 50s maybe, with a goatee beard. He did look vaguely Asian, but was more likely to be Middle Eastern, I decided. His hair was grey but his face was surprisingly unwrinkled; his skin almost glowed.

"That's OK. Anyone would have done the same."

"I don't think so, boy, not these days, not in these times." He grasped my arm, weighed me up for a moment and then lowered his voice to a whisper and said "Here, I want you to have these. They're very tasty, quite unique and entirely vegan." The tramp handed me a small box containing small boiled sweets. It was covered in strange markings, similar to runes.

"I'm okay, thanks."

"Please. Have them on me."

"Oh, okay. Thank you."

"My pleasure."

"Hey," said Mark. "Are we going to make this gig or not?"

"Yeah, come on Tom," said Matt. "Get with the programme."

"OK, I'm coming."

I shook the old boy's hand and told him to take care.

"You're a good boy, God bless you."

***

"WE were like the Avengers in there," Matt laughed as we walked to the venue.

"Yeah, that's us, the Guardians of the…oh shit, I can't think of a word even a bit like Galaxy," said Kez.

"Galactose?" I suggested, handing out the sweets.

"The guardians of sugar?" laughed Mark. "Here, let me just run that past Stan Lee…and it's a no from him."

"Galactus?"

"Galago?" said Kez. "It's a kind of bushbaby."

"These sweets are good," said Matty. "A bit fiery…"

"Gallifrey?" suggested Mark.

"No! Doctor Who would sue. Guardians of the Galloway, of the alley way, of the insanity…nope, it's not working," I said.

"If we were superheroes what powers would we have?" asked Mark.

"I'd be super-cosy," smiled Kez. "My powers would involve lying on the settee eating popcorn, watching box sets and chillaxing."

"I'd have the ability to teleport into Tulisa's shower at will," grinned Matt. "Or the power to freeze time at football when you need a lash."

"Be serious."

"Okay, I'd be The Bull," Matt said decisively. "Part man, part bull…able to charge through any barrier without physical injury."

"All bull!" sniped Kez.

"All horn!" he replied with a smirk.

"What about, Tom?" asked Mark.

"He'd be Time Killer," Matt decided. "I know because I've watched him crucify chronology at work. And you Mark, you'd be…Auto Boy!"

"I don't drive!"

"No not auto as in cars. You can't tell me you're not somewhere on the autistic scale."

"Very funny!"

"Okay how about Sarky Man?" sniped Kez. "Although I'm not sure super-sarcasm counts as much of a power…"

"Thank you Catty Woman! I'd rather have the power to take over people's bodies and be them for as long as I wanted…"

"Like Deadman," I said.

"Yes a bit!" said Mark. "But unlike Boston Brand, I wouldn't use my power to hunt a mysterious one-armed killer, I'd slip into Brad Pitt just as he was about to slip into Angelina."

"Gross," snorted Kez.

"Kez would have to be Lady Luck," I said, steering the conversation away from filth. "Her power would be an uncanny ability to manipulate fortune, good or bad, to her advantage."

"Wait," said Mark solemnly. "We're not Guardians, we're retaliators. All join hands!"

"Weird," muttered Matt.

"We'd be Nemesis!" Mark announced, as we complied. "Channelling divine retribution against all that's evil or unholy!"

"Gee," Matt sniped. "I had my hopes set on Three Men & A Lucky Lady."

Keziah laughed so much she started choking.

"Not so lucky now, is she?" laughed Mark, as he slapped her back.

"Where did get these sweets?" asked Kez as she recovered.

"From the guy, from the old boy we saved..."

"You've given me sweets from a tramp?" Kez turned on me in mock horror, spitting out what was left of it and theatrically wiping her mouth. "You absolute dobber!"

"They taste great," I said defensively.

"They taste like rancid cat's poo."

"I won't even start to ask how you know that," Mark smiled.

"Here we are chaps," Matt announced in the nick of time. "The bar..."

***

THE gig wasn't up to much. The sound system was lousy, the Toerags were all over the place like spilt milk and the beer was watered-down.

"Even the girls are rough," moaned Matt.

"Have a good look at their tattoos though," laughed Mark. "I think one or two of them might even be spelt right."

"Listen to yourselves," laughed Kez. "You are so last century."

"She's pretty though," I said.

"Who?"

I pointed at a tall young woman with a long light brown mane, biker's jacket, leather mini-skirt, fishnet tights and stiletto heels.

"That one in the leather jacket at the bar who looks like a young Tricia Helfer. She's stunning. She turned up a couple of moments ago. I smiled at her and I swear she smiled back."

"So what are you waiting for?" asked Mark.

"Get stuck in," said Matt.

"What should I say?"

"Go up and ask to buy her a drink," said Mark.

"Should I?" I looked at Keziah.

"Yes go on," she said, without much enthusiasm.

"Okay." I took out another sweet.

"Umm, the sweet taste of hobo, the way to any girl's heart…" said Kez.

I smiled wanly and walked towards the bar.

"Is he always so shy with girls?" Keziah asked.

"He's got an embarrassing problem," Mark had replied.

"Yeah," agreed Matt solemnly. "He's got the big V."

"What's that, an STI?" Kez pulled a face.

"No," Matt chuckled. "Virginity."

Moments later I was back.

"No joy?" asked Mark.

"I missed her. By the time I got there she'd gone to the side door over by the stage, and I couldn't get in there cos it's the dressing room. I had a word with the roadie and he says her name is Freeje and she's going out with the lead singer with the headlining band…"

"Frankie and the Blowfish," said Mark.

"Is she blowing Frankie?" asked Matt.

"Probably."

"Freeje…? As long as she's not Free-jid," laughed Matt. "She sounds Swedish, Tom."

"Oh boy!" I replied.

"Oh gawd," laughed Mark.

"Oh well," said Kez, changing the subject. "Shall we stay for them or get a ride back with Priyan? His Dad's picking him up at 11pm."

"His Dad's picking him up?" scoffed Mark. "That's very rock n roll, innit? Very punk."

"Will we all fit?" I asked.

"Yeah, he's got a people carrier."

"Oh yes, Anarchy in the UK," Mark laughed.

"We might as well, it'll save getting taxis at the other end," said Kez.

"You coming, Tom, or are you staying up here with your mates in cardboard city?" asked Matt.

"Tres droll."

"Rock 'n droll, that's us," said Mark. "Come on, we can see the Blowfish another time."

"Maybe Tom the mighty Time Killer wants to hang about and gawp at the Mystery Rock Chick," grinned Matt.

"Oi, leave him be," said Kez.

"Yeah, leave off," I agreed.

"If anyone's going to take the Mick out of him it's me."

"Thanks Kez."

"We can't take the Mick out of him," said Matt. "Nature beat us to it."

"Ho bloody ho."

"A bloody 'ho'? I thought you liked her."

"Give me strength."

Priyan's father Siva dropped me off first. It was only 11.30pm. I crept up to the bathroom and looked at my bruised ribs in the mirror. Not too bad. By the time I'd turned on the laptop, Keziah was on Facebook.

'You OK, Tom?'

'Yeah. Fanx for 2night. Where d'you learn to use a cane like that?'

'Daredevil. LOL'

'You shda driven it thru his black heart.'

'Yeah, if he had one.'

'He had x-eyes.'

'And halitosis.'

'PMSL!'

'Did I tell you about this new funfair opening, Rock World?'

'That sounds cool...no-one will ever say."
"Ouch, I just cut myself on your sarcasm."
'LOL. What u doin?'
'Gonna find something funny on Netflix. Nighty nite.'
'Sweet dreams, luvva-boy.'
'You too, tiger.'
'Grroowwllllllll.'

In the event I spent ten minutes peering at the Maiden poster and prodding it gingerly. It was definitely paper, the flames didn't burn and no-one whispered my name. Daft. Nothing had happened. Imagine if the pictures and posters could really pull me in. I was more likely to get lumbered with trolls, wolves or dorky Orcs than of finding out if Calista really flocked hard.

Enter Sandman

Ozzy Osbourne laughed in my face that night. Except it wasn't Ozzy, it was a fat troll with his features twisted into an approximation of the antique rock star's face. The creature was as hairy as Chewbacca; but up close I could see it was covered in weeping sores. "Sort of Oozy Osbourne," I thought hazily as I recoiled.

The Oz-Troll had lidless eyes and heavy, drooping jowls. Its upper body was too broad for its little legs and its breath smelt rank, like Frank Gallagher's under-pants stewed in meths. "Christ, Oz, have you been gargling with goat urine?" I asked. The creature laughed, exposing a set of jagged, yellow fangs that looked like decaying bullets, and produced his pockmarked scrotum from the dirty loincloth that hung loosely around his middle.

Each of creature's testes was the size of a tennis ball, and there were three of them. "I'm ET," the Oz-Troll announced. "The Extra-Testicle..."

The Oz-Troll was squeezing his exposed gonads so tightly that they had begun to pop out of his body. One...two...three, then another three, then three more...As they hit the ground, each testicle transformed into one of the dancing babies from Ally McBeal; all nine of them moving together in perfect symmetry to a beat only they could hear.

I glanced back towards the troll who had now morphed into Calista Flockhart, but she/he/it was so thin that her skin was translucent and as she glided in front of the babies, her internal organs began moving in rhythm to the song that I could now faintly hear. It was something real old and odd, something my uncle used to play. That's it! It was Hocus Pocus by Focus. Yeah. Rock and yodelling, going together like ice cream and gravy.

The babies formed a kind of singing pyramid under the marmalade sky, with Calista at the apex. As they reached the yodels the creature's face began to swell, becoming redder and redder. With her stick-like body, she looked like a strawberry lollipop.

"Help me," she pleaded in a voice as feeble as a neglected pensioner on a hospital trolley. "Help me, Tommy."

"How?" I said.

"Squeeze my head of course. You must. You must. I'm Ally McBoil, can't you tell?"

Even in the dream I grimaced. "McBoil?" I said. "That is so sad…"

The music stopped. She jumped down and faced me. I hesitated.

"Please squeeze me," she whined. "Squeeze me, please me. Please, Tommeee. Do it for Ally."

Gingerly I put her head between my hands and pressed firmly.

"Harder!" she snapped.

I increased the pressure and her skull popped instantly, splattering me with warm pus.

Then I woke up.

I Don't Like Mondays

Day Four. "What's up, lad? Tired of working for your living already?" The words boomed out in an echo chamber several miles above my head, hanging heavy in the Monday morning air until their vinegary sarcasm soaked in, jerking me reluctantly away from the latest issue of *Vive Le Rock*.

I glanced up into Brian Clarkson's weary sultana eyes, and panicked. I stuffed the mag into my desk drawer, ripping its cover in the process. The pile of files on my left swayed ominously, and then collapsed, scattering its contents across the floor like a paper chase.

A doodlebug of dust exploded in my face. I sneezed. Clarkson sneered. Cue yet another "hard work/honest living/sober life" lecture from my pious walrus of a boss.

For all his Oliver Hardy girth, Clarkson delivered his Calvinist platitudes in a squeaky little Laurel of a voice, which gave his sermons an unavoidably comic side-effect. It didn't help that the suit he was wearing was the colour of wet cement. The bloke was as fat as Friar Tuck and just as stylish.

"This is no laughing matter, Scrimshaw," Clarkson snapped, those narrow eyes aglow with anger. "You will have to learn to take your responsibilities more seriously or else I can tell you..." He leaned forward so that I caught the full force of his breath. Hmm. Tuna. Either that or he was closer to Miss Simms than I'd imagined. "You'll be looking for another job, and let's see you laugh at that."

Clarkson's chubby features regained their usual air of vacant importance as he wombled off. I opened my mouth and closed it again. Git. I mimed firing a Lugar in the Walrus's direction, then grinned as I realised it would take an elephant gun to drop him.

"You OK, T?" whispered Matt, who was delivering the morning post.

"I'm OK, it's Clarky who ought to be worried."

"Eh?"

"The nerve of him! I mean, look at him. He is nothing outside of this office. The clothes he's wearing were out of date when Captain Mainwaring was a Corporal. One day I'm gonna, I'm gonna..."

"What? What you gonna do? Fire him out of a cannon?"

I paused. "It's difficult to talk bullshit when you're gargling with paperclips," I said finally with what I fancied was a large helping of South London menace.

Matt guffawed. "Listen to Mr Lock Stock," he said. "Listen why don't we have a proper beer on Friday, just to cheer you up a bit?"

"Works for me!"

Commuter In A Stupor

I WAS going to have to sort myself out, I decided, as I jogged up the stairs at Waterloo East. Maybe if I rang the GP's surgery tomorrow morning I could get an appointment by the middle of next month.

I'd wasted a few minutes looking for the old tramp, so I'd missed my normal train. Except I hadn't; the 5.16 had been cancelled and consequently the 5.46 was heaving. My carriage was as packed as a group of WAGS on holiday. It couldn't be any more crowded, I decided, without breaking all the known laws of physics, and several of the unknown ones. Sardines would have complained about the crush, and Japanese commuters would have agreed with them.

I was lucky to get a seat; well, half a seat, really. The other half was occupied by a jovial but asthmatic 18-stone dumpling of a woman eating a jumbo packet of Pickled Onion Space Raiders whose hefty buttocks spread like butter in a hot pan. She was here most evenings, as were the two secretaries who giggled and chirped like cartoon chipmunks, the dude with the MP3 player you could hear over his head-phones and the thin-faced middle-aged bore with the clipped Estuary accent who despite reading the *Express* had been known to share intimate details of his home life that Jeremy Kyle would consider far too intimate. He looked like the kind of bloke who'd wear socks with sandals at a water park.

The automated recording kicked in – "This is the 17.46 train to Dartford, calling at Waterloo East, Hither Green…" I started to nod off until Biffo, a building worker whose beer belly was looming above me, stopped shouting into his mobile long enough to start sneezing. The man was one of life's bazookas, exploding with loud passion at every possible opportunity.

I knew his name was Biffo because he started every conversation with the words "Oi, oi, Biffo 'ere, 'ow's it 'angin'?" before talking loudly about nothing until he lost service somewhere near Borough Market.

What came first, I wondered unkindly. The mobile or the lobotomy? Then I hated myself for being a snob.

I took shelter behind a discarded copy of the Metro and grimaced. The only interesting things in the entire rag were an advertising feature for a new funfair called Rock World opening down at Ramsgate, and a half-page advert for an Ozzy Osbourne concert. I shut my eyes and slipped fitfully into the arms of Morpheus.

In my dream, the Oz-Troll returned to haunt me, only this time when I squeezed Ally's head I didn't wake up. For a moment all I could see were colours: fiery reds, hyacinth blue, jade and emerald greens, deep purple and sulphur yellow. But as the psychotic rainbow calmed down, an eerie landscape formed. I strained my eyes against the lingering marmalade glow of the sky. There was a figure on a hillock about thirty feet in front of me. I squinted. It was a nun with Tricia Helfer's face, beckoning to me. Freeje! I moved towards her and the stones beneath my feet came alive. Each one I stepped on sang out in pain. The faster I moved, the louder they screamed. It was a horrible racket; child-like and unsettling, like the death agony of Iggle Piggle being roasted alive. I slapped my hands over my ears to try and blot out the sound.

Freeje gave a gentle soothing laugh and the screaming stopped. I could see her properly now, standing proud against the lime-speckled clouds – great cheek bones, pert breasts, flat stomach, legs that could melt a cheese sandwich from 25 yards and shoulder-length hair framing eyes full of spirit. She gave me a smile that managed to be open and half-crazed at the same time. Naturally I ignored the crazy side.

I was, if truth be told, I was already aroused. My manhood had sprung up like an exclamation mark.

I started running again and suddenly my path was blocked by a second nun, an exact double of Freeje. But this one winked and morphed straight into the Oz-Troll. WTF...

"Tit wank?" the creature asked unpleasantly, flashing fatty man-breasts that had teeth where her nipples should be. The exclamation mark twisted into a question mark, and immediately wilted.

"YOU wanna FUCK me like an ANIMAL!" the creature yelled. "You like to BURN me on the INSIDE!"

"No!" my dream self snapped. "That's not your song, that's Limp Bizkit."

"What ya gonna do about it?" it snarled. "Slash my ass with a chain-saw?"

I looked deep into my tormentor's dark hateful eyes and whacked it, hard. It seemed to do the trick. The creature shrieked and limped off towards a railway sign that simply said New Cross. A tidal wave of electric guitar feedback exploded out of nowhere, like Jimi Hendrix conjuring up a celestial purple haze.

As I ran forward I seemed to be growing taller, broader, and stronger. I could feel my biceps expanding, ripping through my shirt, like Popeye after he'd downed a shed-load of spinach. My shoes had become leather boots, my shirt an armoured breastplate. My trousers had gone, and instead I was wearing one of those warrior tunics the heroes had on in Jason & The Argonauts. A splendid two-handed sword appeared to be hanging at my side in a leather scabbard. I didn't have time to figure it out, though. I'd reached her.

"Tiwaz," she said.

"Eh?"

"Take me..."

Hendrix faded away and Iron Maiden roared into life. She started to kiss me and I eagerly responded, thrusting my tongue into her gorgeous gob. Something was wrong, though. Freeje's mouth was flimsy and weak, giving way to my tongue as if it were a switchblade slicing through a peach. It was repulsive but I

27

couldn't pull away, not even when her left eye popped out and her face caved in on me...

Freeje was turning to slush in my arms.

"Melter, melter, thought he had a belter," mocked someone...the Oz-Troll? I threw up then and there, my vomit blending with the stinking syrup of her decomposition. What was left of her splattered my legs, burning into my skin like sulphuric acid.

The front of my body felt like it was on fire.

Iron Maiden had gone. The only sound in my ears was a wolf howling for what seemed like minutes. Then "Help me Tommy," a woman cried.

I felt a hand on my shoulder, shaking me roughly. And that was when the distinctly unfeminine voice told me "Oi mate, ain't this your stop?" Thanks Biffo.

When I got home I realised my crisp white shirt was covered in such a mess of colours it made a Jackson Pollock picture look monotone.

That night, I told Mark and Matt everything, and immediately regretted it. Firstly because they couldn't work out why it was happening either; and secondly because they kept secrets the way a cuckoo clock keeps quiet. But we agreed to meet the next day in the pub near my office for what Mark called a proper discussion and Matt called a bloody good session.

The Dark Lantern

Day Five. The women in the Dark Lantern always talked about soap operas and sex; it was a compulsive disorder. The soap bored me to tears, but the sauce always titillated. The barmaids were radiant and beautiful, unobtainable Cockney goddesses. My favourite was Natalie – "Nat'lee" - Barker, the buxom, copper-haired 19-year-old who was currently pouring me a diet coke and jabbering on about last night's dollop of EastEnders TV woe.

I caught myself staring at the cross pendant that nestled at the top of her cleavage. I'd noticed it before, of course, but now it had started to throb and grow and I couldn't look away. To my horror, I felt my eyeballs begin to physically stretch out from their sockets as if I were a cartoon character. I lifted my hands to my face. My eyes were on stalks the size of jumbo sausages.

"What is she on about, not Dead-Enders again?" Matt broke the spell. My eyeballs snapped back into place, and then span around like the symbols of a fruit machine that had just been given a mighty yank by The Hulk. They stopped with such force it's a wonder I didn't shoot pound coins out of my arse. He didn't seem to notice.

"Yeah, Dot Cotton's gorn lipstick lesbian I think," I joked lamely. My eyes were stinging.

"Even Natalie wouldn't buy that. Here Nat, sling us one of your ham rolls, please. Is that funny orange-faced slapper still in it? The one who looks like a Satsuma."

"Oi, don't you start on Kat," Natalie protested, handing over the last roll of the day.

"I heard Roxy Mitchell's leaving soon cos she's got trouble with her legs. Her knees have got different postcodes."

"Sexist pig," Natalie snapped.

I grinned weakly. The thought that Nat had spiked my drink in order to have her wicked way with me flashed through my mind agreeably if not entirely convincingly.

"You eating, Tom?" Matt asked.

"I was going to have the all-day breakfast."

"Order it in rhyming slang…"

"What? No."

"Come on, see if Nat gets it."

"Oh okay, give us a second…,"

Matt was Bermondsey born and bred. To him, Blackheath was the countryside. He'd been tutoring me in the arcane mysteries of underground London lingo since I'd started work.

"Right," I said finally. "Two coat-hangers please Nat, a scotch peg, Stephened to perfection, some stars and garters, and two serial slashers…"

"Right," Nat replied, unfazed. "That's two sausages, a fried egg, fried toms and two rashers of bacon. Is there anything else sir needs?"

"Apart from a look at Nat's Walters," laughed Matt.

"I need some Holy Ghost please."

"Amen," said Matt as a shimmering vision of Freeje materialised behind the bar and smiled at me.

"Right," he said. "Let's talk about these dreams."

"What dreams?" asked Natalie. "Bet they're wet ones."

"Well it's one dream really, he gets the same one every night," Matt said. I shot him a don't-talk look which he naturally ignored.

"Yeah, all exploding trouser conkers and Ozzy Osbourne."

"Trouser conkers," Natalie giggled.

"Ally McBeal was in there too, and yet he swears he isn't on acid."

"I'd lay off the mushroom soup if I was you, Tommy," she laughed.

"The thing is, in his head he can get inside album posters…"

"How do you mean?"

"He looks at a poster and he can think himself physically inside them, and while most men would dig out Electric Ladyland, Brains here opts for Iron Maiden. I mean, I'd go for the Pussycat Dolls or Girls Aloud as long as I didn't have to hear the music."

"Are girls 'allowed' in your life, Tom?" asked Natalie.

"I, erh…"

"You ever dropped acid Nat?" Matt asked, sparing my blushes.

"Never. How about you?"

"Someone put mescaline in my drink at a party. I could see all these monkeys coming out of the wall. Very friendly monkeys they were too. When I snapped out of it, I was disappointed that they weren't really there. I can even remember their names. There was one called Dave, two Micks and a Peter."

He paused. Natalie looked at him blankly.

"You're not getting this are you? One Dave, two Micks, a Peter...the Monkees?" Mick started to sing "cheer up sleepy Jean, oh what can it mean..."

No reaction.

"They were a band, Nat."

"Before my time."

"And before mine, obviously. But what kind of excuse is that? Wagner was before my time but it don't mean I don't start to tingle every time I hear the Ride of The Valkyries."

"The who?"

"No, that was My Generation."

"You've lost me."

"I'll get you a download. What's your mobile number?"

"Nice try, sunshine."

Matt chuckled and went back to the fruit machines.

"Did you see what he did there?" Nat asked me.

I nodded. I could see I'd nodded because I was up on the ceiling watching my body below. I watched my hand lift my drink and sip it. I saw my tongue roll one of the tramp's sweets round my mouth and my blush come and go unbidden. If I was down there, what was the 'me' up here? My spirit?

I tried to will myself back into my physical shell but nothing happened; it was like I was glued to the plasterwork. I was powerless. Until Mark strolled into the pub and spoke to me...

"All right, Tom. Sorry I'm late, I had to deliver a parcel down the road."

My inner self was immediately pulled back into my physical form.

"Blimey, who sucked the jam out of your donut?"

"Aw, you know how it is."

"Ah, right, the dream, good, let's get started."

I nodded. A white lie seemed a lot easier than the truth.

"Exploding testicles, that's weird enough. But Ally McBoil? That's proper lame, mate."

"It's not me making this up, Mark. Well not directly. It's my subconscious. I can't exercise any quality control on the gags."

"And Tiwaz, you say? Not Tiswas? The old kids show Chris Tarrant used to do?"

"I've never even heard of Tiswas," I said glumly.

"Have you tried googling Tiwaz?"

"Of course. I got a pagan metal band and some guff about Elder Futhark."

"Hmm. All about as clear as a Pete Doherty urine sample."

"Elder Futhark? Didn't her persecute Bugs Bunny?" joked Matt.

"Leave it out, Matty," I groaned. "The point is I hate dreams. Especially in films, books or TV shows. They're a really hackneyed plot device. Nothing matters in dreams, there's no internal logic, no sense of reality. So for me to be tormented by the same piece of shit nightmare day after day is like, I dunno, a grammar pedant getting trapped in a room full of badly punctuated greengrocer's signs and Slade set-lists."

"You poor dear, I feel your pain," said Matt, who clearly didn't. "It must be hell for you, upset by dreams. What are you, six?"

"It's the indignity of Ozzy Osbourne's gonads that upsets him," opined Mark. "At least Balzac's ball-sack would have a little intellectual credibility. And you are a bit of a human comedy these days if I'm truthful."

"Do you think it could be astral projection?" asked Matt.

"What into a dream? How does that work?" I replied glumly. "A dream with melting women and me throwing up…"

"Maybe it's astral projectile vomit," sniggered Mark.

"Shocking."

"Sounds like you need a neurologist."

"How about trying dream analysis if it's really getting you, Tom?" Matt suggested almost helpfully.

"A racket," grunted Mark. "You'd be better off asking Mystic Meg."

"Well, I'd go to a professional therapist," said Matt. "I mean if it was good enough for Tony Soprano."

"Maybe…" I said, changing the subject. "Did Kez tell you about the new funfair opening down at Ramsgate?"

"No."

"It's called Rock World, it's got a rock 'n' roll theme, obviously."

"Obvs. Maybe they'll have a Bryan Ferris wheel," said Mark.

"And Marc Bolan bumper cars," Matt chimed in.

"Or maybe a drugs store that actually sells drugs."

"I'm hoping for a Marilyn Manson Chamber of Horrors," I said. "Or some kind of Alice Cooper themed 'death rollercoaster'."

"I think they've got that at Alton Towers," said Matt.

"Talking of horrors, I just saw on Twitter that the Blowfish are playing a charity gig down Deptford tomorrow night if you fancy it," Mark said. "And if it's Deptford, *she* might be there..."

"Yeah, could be good. Listen I'd better get back to work. I don't want to wind up the Walrus."

"Cheer up, Tom mate," said Matty, pretending to sympathise. "It could be worse. You could dream that you're trapped in Albert Square and never wake up."

"Oh here he goes again," said Natalie. "Oi, you! Here Tommy, why don't you try watching Sex & The City before you go akip. You might have better dreams."

She leant forward so I could see the white of her bra down the top of her blouse. The cross pendent fell forward, glinting and growing drawing my eyes back to her bust. "Which one do you fancy then?"

I felt myself blush again. I was about to say they both looked splendid when Natalie added: "I bet it's the blonde one, Samantha."

I nodded, uncertainly.

"She's a right slapper!"

Shit. I never get it right.

"I'd better get going," I said.

"See you later, alligator," grinned Mark.

"Yeah laters," said Matt.

"He's weird," I heard Natalie whisper. "He's always staring at my knockers."

"Well be fair they're worth staring at Nat," said Matt. "Sling us another swift pint, gorgeous."

I later discovered that after I'd gone, Mark and Matt, my so-called friends filled Natalie in on my inexperience with women and how embarrassed I got when the barmaids talked dirty. This Quisling-like betrayal would have enormous consequences, which I'll get to in good time. I didn't go back to work that day. I hopped on a bus and got Mum to phone in claiming I'd had an asthma attack. I panicked at half four though when Mum said the office were on the line. I still-paused the X Files re-run and picked up the portable extension as breathlessly as possible. It was only Matt.

"Best you rest mate," he said. "I was only telling Miss Simms here how pasty you were looking in the health food bar at lunch time."

"Don't drop me in it, Matt."

"S'alright mate. Old Iron Draws had a hospital appointment and Clarkson's up in a meeting on the ninth floor all afternoon so no-one has even noticed you're not here. The reason I phoned is I was telling my brother Steve about your dream…"

"How many more people are you going to tell?"

"Listen, Steve is the brains of the family. He's studying history at Warwick. Anyway he's worked part of it out."

"Go on."

"He says Tiwaz is an ancient Saxon god and that the growling at the end is probably Fernir, the wolf who Tiwaz battled in Saxon mythology."

"But I've never heard of Tiwaz."

"Maybe not, or maybe you read about him and the memory is suppressed in your subconscious. Any way, it all fits. The clothes you're wearing, the sword. It all makes sense."

"And the woman?"

"No idea. It's probably just your rampant virgin subconscious sexing it up."

"Did he have any idea how I can turn the dream off?"

"He did say one thing. Every night it's the same dream, right? You know what's going to happen. So tonight before you sleep visualise something else, concentrate on the dream events taking a different course, don't squeeze Ally's head, don't snog the girl. And if her mince pie still falls out, maybe you could get her to wink you off."

"Ha, ha," I said miserably.

"Seriously mate, Steve thinks your conscious mind can defuse your subconscious."

"Worth a try."

"Well don't be too grateful."

"Sorry Matty, drinks on me tomorrow night."

"I really don't get why you're so pissed off about this, mate. If you're just dreaming it all, no harm done. If it's for real, and you're really transporting into artwork and photos, you've got yourself a super-power."

"I guess…"

"So enjoy it while you can! Master it! Check out Battlestar Galactica posters from the inside if that floats your boat, or do what I'd do and splash out on a copy of Nuts, with the emphasis on splashing…"

"You mean…"

"I do."

"I hadn't thought…"

"But you will. Laters, skiver."

I looked over at my bedroom wall. The Charge of the Scots Greys at Waterloo looked properly daunting, but Connie-Lyn from Loaded she might be worth a visit…

Wednesday's Child

Day Six. It had been a quiet day at work, Matty had a day off and I'd kept my head down and avoided the Lantern. I was standing on Waterloo East station when Matt rang.

"How'd it go, bro?"

"What?"

"The vital scientific research you had to do with a jazz mag yesterday."

"Not yet. I will, when the mood takes me."

"Hello! Is that the right number? I wanted Tommy Scrimshaw. I seem to have got through to the Anti-Sex League."

"Leave it out…"

"You certainly have."

"Yeah. Listen I've gotta go Matt, the train's here."

I joined my fellow commuters fighting for a seat in my usual carriage. At least I got a whole one as Madam Sumo was sitting opposite me. Today she was wearing a Sponge Bob Squarepants t-shirt and snacking on a bag of Flamin' Hot Monster Munch. And just my luck – Biffo the burly building worker still had a head full of cold and no handkerchief.

He sneezed loudly, like a hippo having an orgasm. Sponge Bob's smile turned into a disconcerting grimace. Maybe he's got allergies, I thought. He certainly seems allergic to basic hygiene. I would have said something if the guy hadn't been twice my age and three times my size.

"God bless you," said the fat woman, spraying me with a second coat of half-chewed Monster Munch.

"They do say that when you sneeze your heart stops for a split second," observed the thin man in his clipped Estuary English. "And if you sneeze at the point of climax as my wife has done on more than one occasion, you may need urgent medical assistance. Why only last weekend…"

Sponge Bob hid his eyes and even Biffo looked aghast. Groaning internally, I put in my iPod ear-phones. The automated recording kicked in – "This is the 17.46 train to Dartford, calling at Waterloo East, Hither Green, Bifrost, Asgard…" What? What was that? I took out the ear-phones as the rather posh female recording continued "Mottingham, New Eltham, Sidcup…" Don't tell me I'm hearing things now too! Glumly, I pressed play on the Old Firm Casuals and turned to face the rain-splattered window. What would you say to God if you met him and he sneezed on you, I wondered? I spotted a rainbow as I drifted into yet another bloody dream, this time involving an ancient feast presided over by some old beardie bloke with a raven perched on each shoulder. He looked deep in thought. Another younger fellow holding a hammer walked up and whispered in his ear. Beardie stared straight down the rainbow and into my eyes. "Tiwaz," he said simply, at which point Biffo the builder sneezed violently. Just as well as we were a minute out of Sidcup.

There was still a rainbow over the train as I left the station, but it sure as hell wouldn't lead to a heavenly party. Why wasn't brown in the rainbow, anyway? What did God have against brown? I walked into the Chinese takeaway up the hill for some ribs. The sight of all that Norse nosh had left me hungry. And yeah, it was Norse. The old chap with the ravens must have been Odin and the hammer holder was Thor.

If this was just my subconscious rehashing Viking mythology, I'd be gutted. Talk about old hat! Marvel had done all that to death.

***

We'd agreed to meet in the Deptford club where Frankie & The Blowfish were opening for The Bishops, a punk band from North London with a notoriously violent following. But the doormen laughed at Mark and my fake IDs and refused to let us in. I texted Kez who came out to join us, just as Matt was turning up.

"Just as well you didn't get in," she said.

"Why?" asked Mark.

"Cos guess who the lead singer of the Bishops is?"

"No idea," said Matt.

"The monkey who Thomas took on last weekend Joey Bishop, the twat who wanted us to remember his name but looked like he'd be hard-pressed to spell it..."

"Close escape."

"And their mob looked even meaner and dumber than he did."

"Was she in there?" I asked.

"Who?"

"The Blowfish beauty," laughed Mark.

"I didn't notice," Keziah lied.

"You're lucky the big lump didn't spot you," said Matt.

"You know me, in and out like a shadow."

"Especially when it comes to buying a round," laughed Mark.

"Oi, you. I'm out of pocket because you little boys don't look old enough to get into an eighteen-plus venue. I bought a ticket. So by my reckoning the drinks are on you."

"When will I ever get to see her, now?" I moaned.

"Tom, mate," said Matt. "Do us a favour. Go home and come back when your head's not in fairyland."

"Thanks for your support, chaps."

"I'm only serious."

"He's joking Tom," said Keziah.

"No, he's right. I'm no use to anyone in this mood. You go on. I'll sort myself out in time for next weekend."

"Want me to come back with you and hang a bit?" Keziah asked.

"No, you're OK. Have fun." I walked off to the distant bus stop and missed the next part of the conversation when Mark laughed and said: "He has no idea, has he?"

And Kez replied: "No idea of what?"

"That you fancy the pants off him."

"You breathe a word Mark Gladbury and I'll never speak to you again," Keziah has said. "And that goes for you too, Matt Cluer."

"OOOOOOO!!!" they said as one. "HAND BAG!!!!!!"

If Keziah had rolled her eyes any harder she'd have been looking at her cerebral cortex.

***

That night I sat in my room reading until 11pm and then watched old comedy repeats on Dave. When I finally turned in, I thought every aspect of my nightmare through the way I wanted it to go. In this version, the woman didn't melt in my arms. We made sweet love, and then I beheaded the Oz-Troll and ran the wolf through. Lovely job.

In the event I dreamed about something entirely different; something very random indeed. I dreamt US late night TV comedians David Letterman and Jay Leno were blitzing one-liners at each other, and talking about me…

Fire, I'll Take You To Burn

Day Seven. From my desk I could see Clarkson talking to Phyllis Simms. He'd better watch his step with me from now on. By day I might be mild-mannered Thomas Scrimshaw but by night I was a Saxon god. Yeah, Tiwaz, warrior metal king! Slayer of tyrants! Righter of wrongs! Deflowerer of damsels (pending)! Sir Lancelot on a souped-up Harley…why in my dreams I could splatter him across her glass partition like a fly on a windscreen.

"Tom? Post up, day-dreamer." Matt handed me an empty envelope with a book hidden underneath it. The book was Gods And Myths Of Northern Europe. "Stevie sent me this for you. He says there's a bit in here about Tiwaz and Fenrir. According to him, your dream mission, should you accept it, is to take on and defeat Fenrir who is the adversary of the gods. He says Tiwaz was a war god of great bravery and that you will succeed but you'll lose a hand in the process. Probably your wanking hand…That'll leave you stumped."

"Cool, thanks mate."

"Here and this will give you a giggle," Matt slipped me the latest Human Resources announcement, freshly torn from the canteen notice board. The headline was 'Transgender Opportunities'. I smiled. The Authority's Human Rights co-ordinator – a transvestite called Colin/Chloe who often wore a skirt to work – issued strange proclamations concerning equality, multiculturalism or lesbian outreaching on a regular basis. In the summer they'd started a Low Self-Esteem Group which met in the local community hall. Some puerile wag, almost certainly Matt, had added 'Enter by back-door' on every leaflet.

"Watch out," he said. "Clarkson's about." Reluctantly, I cleared up my paper work as Matt scurried off. Clarkson was still talking to, or rather at, Miss Simms but they were now on the move. Simms seemed to love the sound of his droning voice almost as much as he did and tittered at his smug asides. Her laugh was brittle, like glass breaking.

She was a plump bespectacled woman, with sensible shoes, a pleated checked skirt and a mauve blouse buttoned to the neck. Her grey-hair was razored so fiercely into her neck that she could have come straight from a casting for a new prison warden on Orange Is The New Black.

I had no idea what manner of undergarments lurked beneath those protective layers, but it was a fair bet they hadn't come from the Paris branch of Fifi Chachnil.

Not for nothing was my current favourite track Something More Than This by the Aussie band Marching Orders. Groaning inwardly, I made a great show of sorting out the files and studying them intensely. The top one contained detailed references to some long forgotten meeting about dog-catching (nearly one third of the annual budget of £139,700 was eaten up by 'the cost of democracy', which translates into English as plain old red-tape).

Over the three months since I'd been working for the Authority, I had checked and processed all the regulations relating to questions and points of order for meetings since 1995, including umpteen different committees, sub-committees and ad-hoc working groups. I had compiled all the rules governing parking in the car park, complete with detailed annotations about every single recorded violation. Now I was due to start a similar tiresome log detailing every incident of staff sickness over a similar period. My work wasn't just tedious; it was by definition inconsequential because Clarkson's department had been specifically set up to supervise the collation of information so insignificant that no room could be found for it on the Authority's computer data base. The department continued to exist because there was a provision for it in the budget, and there was a provision for it in the budget because it continued to exist. The logic was as circular as it was self-serving.

The system was, Matt had once told me, designed to make the Authority function more like the European Commission, universally derided by the thoughtful as a complete and utter chaotic disaster.

I had long since given up any attempt to reason with the mass of useless trivia it was my job to accumulate. When I had first started work there I'd tried to talk to Miss Simms about the irrelevance of it all, but had quickly learnt that such conversations were taboo, sacrilegious even. Her career like Clarkson's was based on the file. His aura of supercilious superiority, as blatant and out-dated as his aftershave, depended on it. It was his livelihood and his God and he served it faithfully. To question any part of it was to undermine the whole spider's web of power and vested interests that was spun around it. You might as well expect him to question his own existence. And so the process of storing obsolete information, this plague of paperwork, went on, feeding on itself, creating its own norms and creeds – a huge erection to the creaking inefficiency of modern day bureaucracy – and I kept my thoughts to myself.

A phone rang. As Clarkson answered it I glanced at the clock. 10.42? Was that all? God, there was still over an hour before I could slip out for a lunch break. I wasn't even allowed to use the office email after Simms caught me debating Aquaman's powers with a kid from accounts, specifically how the aquatic superhero could survive for so long on the ocean bed without gills and under so much pressure; which is, I'm sure you'll agree, a perfectly valid scientific inquiry. I drummed my fingers on the desk and glanced up only to catch her and eye and look straight away again. Miss Simms. She ought to call herself Ms, I decided, short for Miserable Old Cow.

I'd begun to suspect Simms wasn't a real person at all but a composite of harridans melded into one monstrous being, with eagle eyes, the hearing of a bat, and a *Sunday Telegraph* editorial for a brain.

It was still 10.42. Really? I want proof. I'm convinced God uses time to torment mankind. It definitely operates at different tempos in and out of work. In work, time moves like a sloth with a hang-over as if eternity was flat-lining, but out of work it seems to run on crystal meth. Out of work time goes so fast it was almost a crime to sleep. An hour in the Dark Lantern lasts the equivalent of five minutes of work time.

It was 10.43. I sucked on one of the tramp's very moreish sweets. Clarkson was still rabbiting away self-importantly to Simms. The look on her face was something close to worship. I glanced back at the clock. 10.43 But, hey…what was up with the hands?

The minute hand and the second hand had drawn themselves out of the clock-face and formed a v-sign aimed straight at me. The hour hand stood up next to them with a placard saying "Thomas Scrimshaw Kills Time! Protest! Go Slow" I blinked and looked back. The clock became bigger and bigger, until it had taken up the entire office wall, and then it began to glow like a miniature sun. I felt my ethereal self being sucked out of my body and into it. Feelings of warmth and well-being flooded into me.

Then the clock shrank back to its normal size with me trapped inside it. But I wasn't looking out into one office, but four, then eight, then a hundred offices. It was as if I were watching a movie where the director had split the screen to keep track of multiple plot developments – except I wasn't seeing different scenes, just many versions of the same one. Or maybe similar ones? There were subtle differences between each tableau. I tried to concentrate on one of the offices. I could see my corporal self slouched over a file at my desk but in this scenario, Clarkson wasn't on the phone he was lecturing me, waving photocopies of various exam certificates in my face as he banged on repeatedly. "You can't get anywhere without qualifications," he was saying. (Not that Clarkson had ever gone anywhere worth going in his entire rotten life... It was even rumoured by some of the more malignant office juniors that he had no home and actually whiled away his nights by digging out old files and running his stubby walrus fingers ecstatically over their dust-lined crevices, while abusing himself.)

In another office scene, Clarkson and Simms were naked and fornicating on her desk like two tons of condemned veal colliding on a ghost-train. Horrible. I turned my eyes to the next. Now I saw Phyllis alone by the filing cabinet changing her thick grey tights for another pair. As she slipped them off I could see her legs for the first time ever. More disturbingly I could see her veins. The veins on Phyllis's legs exploded in vivid Catherine wheels which wove into each other squeezing what was left of her pale skin in to thousands of tiny cells. "Miss Simms has gone Smurfin'," I giggled to myself. "Smurfin' USA…"

On and on I went through the many alternative offices. I saw kindly Clarksons and violent foul-mouthed Clarksons; gay Clarksons, Marxist Clarksons and a masochist Clarkson who seemed to enjoy Simms using his scrotum as an ashtray. The permutations were endless. But try as I might, I couldn't see beyond the office. I couldn't even feast my eyes on the lovely Kirsty who answered the phones in reception...

I tried to make my spirit self glide through the door to where she sat. I concentrated hard, edging slowly down the access stairs. There she was; I could see the back of her head. I coughed. Kirsty turned to greet me and…

BRING! BRING!

My office phone rang. My spirit was sucked out of the clock and back into my body, with the speed and force of an aircraft toilet. Ouch. I picked the phone up and grunted "Yeah?" It was Matt. "Where are you man? It's half-twelve. It's not like it's your round or anything."

I had been inside the clock for nearly two hours.

Baffled, I grabbed my jacket and walked to the pub as briskly as I could manage. I wasn't going to drink today but I needed the company, if only to keep my mind focused on Actual Reality. My head felt woozy.

***

THE Lantern was smart but cosy, all rickety wooden tables and leather-backed chairs, with a friendly old-fashioned atmosphere, although it was pretty empty for a Wednesday. A heavy-breasted Bermondsey girl called Mandy was behind the bar with Natalie. Both women giggled when they saw me and I blushed immediately. Before I could ask for a soda and lime, Matt had ordered me a pint of Stella and carried on berating Natalie about her slimming magazine.

When he went off to play the fruit machine the women started targeting me, talking about their bras, and morning-after pills for men and all sorts of sexual shenanigans that made my face even redder....

"Do you like Mandy's boobs, Tom?" Natalie asked innocently. The answer "compared to what?" flashed through my mind but remained unspoken. Of course I liked her boobs. They were magnificent.

"Very nice," I said, ordering a large scotch in a feeble attempt to look like a sophisticated Dan Draper style man of the world.

"Now I wonder what made you think of a double," she laughed. "You naughty boy. You're right, though, they are nice. You can think of them next time you're bashing the bishop if you like," she said, adding a Barbara Windsor Carry On giggle.

Natalie winked at Mandy and the barmaids went into a pre-arranged routine about sexual preferences. Size, shape, speed, positions...they explored every possible avenue. My face went beyond crimson into a darker shade of beetroot red. I stared intently at a discarded copy of the Sun desperately hoping the women weren't aware of my interest, completely oblivious to the fact that this was all for my benefit. There was a picture of Ricky Gervais on the TV page which suddenly turned and faced me. "They're not going to stop until you run away," he said. I threw the paper back down with a start.

"I'm not keen on it," Natalie was saying. "But if a bloke knows what he's doing I don't mind it. It's all about delicacy; delicacy and lubrication."

Dear God! "Same again please, Nat," I mumbled. I glanced back at the picture of Gervais. He winked at me.

I'm not sure now if it was the drink or the effects of 'doing time' inside the clock but I started to black-out and then fade in and out of consciousness as hallucinatory waves of sound washed over me. I rose unsteadily to my feet, smiled feebly and staggered back to the office, unaware of the barmaids chuckling conspiratorially behind me. I was back at my desk by the time they had stopped laughing.

Clarkson was off at a meeting somewhere, so the office atmosphere wasn't too grim. I went through the motions of work for half an hour before making my regular afternoon visit to the gents. Still wobbly, I locked the cubicle, sat on the seat fully clothed and nodded off. To sleep, perchance to dream...

I had a new Human Resources proclamation ('Celebrate Winterval!') freshly torn from the outside notice on my lap on which I laboriously assembled a roll-up using Artemisia leaves, making myself a tobacco-free herbal "joint" – I couldn't stand fags, and didn't care for the dozy side effects of cannabis. I wouldn't smoke at all if it didn't help pass the time.

I lit up, inhaling deeply and coughed almost immediately. Whether it was the cough or the aroma that caught the attention of the occupant of the neighbouring cubicle I could not say. But Brian Clarkson, for it was he, armed only with a pile of files and a copy of the *Daily Mail*, had his suspicions more aroused than was good for a fat man's heart.

The Walrus dropped to his fat knees, which spread like jelly-fish on the cold tiled floor, and peered under the partition. All he could see were a pair of unpolished brogues. A penny dropped when it should have been spent: any man attending to his proper business would have his trousers round his ankles. Impatience, coupled with suspicion, bred action. He shot out of his cubicle and banged firmly on my door.

"Who is in there?" roared my boss. "Come out this minute."

Shit. I was as caught out and kippered as an enchanted Merino lamb pole-dancing on a vertical rotisserie. Think, Tom. Think innocence, think outraged...

I opened the cubicle door with what I hoped was an indignant expression. Clarkson was having none of it.

"Explain yourself, Scrimshaw," he ranted. "You were idling, weren't you? You were WASTING AUTHORITY TIME. And what's that you're smoking?" He sniffed. "Is it...is it POT?"

I toyed with the idea of claiming it as medical marijuana but instead I merely grinned foolishly.

"Get out of there! What is the meaning of this? You're not fit to work here. Not only are you fired as of this minute but I am going to phone the police immediately. Never in all my life…"

Now I'd had enough. "Poke your job, Mr Clarkson," I said boldly. "Poke your job, poke your Authority and poke your police."

I pushed past my boss, bolted out into corridor and into the stairwell, heading down towards the ground floor. Clarkson followed anxiously, as fast as his tottering frame would allow. I could have kept going but when he reached the bottom and passed the main store room, I couldn't resist the temptation. I burst in and started pushing all of the files off the shelves, coughing as the air filled with dust.

"A small pointless gesture of defiance," said a sardonic Midlands voice behind me. "But not enough, bruv." It was the Oz-Troll, who theatrically flicked his fingers producing a spark of fire which set a pile of papers alight. For a moment it smouldered unnoticed, then came the brilliant burst of flame as 'Processed Expenses, '96 – '97, A-E' went up in smoke. Uh oh. I looked from the fire back at the troll who had vanished.

There was a strange rumbling noise coming from the stairwell. Clarkson? I stepped back into the corridor and looked left. Yep, Clarkson. No. Dozens of Clarksons! A small army of near-identical grey Walrus men were surging towards me, many individuals taking on a collective identity as they united with one common purpose – revenge. And this heaving, seething, roaring abusive phalanx of fear and failure was coming straight at me.

There were fewer dead eyes in a mass grave.

I froze. It was like suburbia was boiling over. Beige rage! These were the dull lifeless people who had inherited the earth with their meagre dreams of a pension-linked new order. They thought that I had put a match to their world and by implication the red-taped middle class impotence it symbolised. They would tear me apart.

Gulping, I turned and fled. The sea of blurred faces bobbed relentlessly behind me, morphing between men and walruses as they moved. I stumbled, falling blinding. Weak wet hands grabbed my legs. In the distance I thought I heard the howl of a wolf. I kicked out wildly and sprawled along the floor, propelling myself down and along. Clutching at a radiator, I pulled myself to my feet again and ran. Ahead of me now was Dugash, looking like Norman Tebbit with toothache. He had adopted a steely, predatory pose and was baring his teeth while fixing me with what he imagined to be a paralysing basilisk stare. From nowhere Darth Vader's theme, The Imperial March from Star Wars, started to swell. It was scary, but not scary enough. I turned my shoulder to greet his chest and sent him flying. Yeah! All those Wednesday afternoons of second team rugby had paid off at last.

My face was dripping with sweat. I could feel the blood throbbing like a Nicko McBrain drum solo around my temples. Suddenly Iron Maiden were playing in my brain: *'Run to the hills/Run for your li-ii-fffeee'*. Somewhere along here there had to be a way out…yeah, there…I saw a fire exit and booted it open, bursting into the daylight…and on I ran, ignoring the alarm bells ringing behind me. I ran until I felt like my whole body was going to explode, and when I couldn't run any more I leant against a wall and tried to catch my breath. I looked behind me. No-one. I'd done it! I was out. I was free.

Free for what? Free to sign on? Great. How was I going to explain this to mum? Right on cue the heavens opened…

Waterloo Sunset

I sheltered in a doorway, sucking what I'd come to think of as a Happy Hobo boiled sweet and waiting for the rain to stop. It was hard to see where the storm clouds ended and my clouds of despondency began. My mobile was switched off and would remain so until after office hours. The last thing I needed now was a telephone bollocking from my former boss. Or Mum. Oh crap. What if Clarkson phoned home and grassed me up? I groaned inwardly. That'd give Mum and Frank something else to row about: "You were always too soft on that boy," "No, your bloody mother lets him get away with murder too…" "Don't you bring my mother in to this…" "She was always round here poking that great hooter of hers in where it wasn't wanted…." "What do you mean, 'great hooter', what was wrong with my mother's nose?" "It was in the middle of that great fat ugly face of hers…"

And if that wasn't bad enough, I'd also have to cope without any income. I had more chance of marrying Rihanna than of getting a decent reference. Fate had well and truly piddled in my pockets this time.

The rain eased up so I walked down to the Embankment. The river always calmed me down, unlike modern London architecture. Much of it deserved to be fire-bombed. Ahead of me was No. 1 Westminster Bridge, a hideous hexagonal monstrosity, derelict and useless, that had squatted like an ugly concrete toad in the middle of the roundabout at the southern end of the bridge for longer than I had been alive. Must look a treat from the London Eye...

The last of the December sun strained through the winter clouds. I looked down at the Thames, quivering like murky jelly by his side. How easy it would be to lose myself in those inviting ripples, to just dive in and end it all. I balanced precariously on the embankment wall. One jump and I'm history. Who'd miss me? No job, no girl, no prospects…suddenly the ancient Sex Pistols anthem fired up in my head, 'No future, no future, no future for yoouuuu…' They'd been Grandad's favourite band too.

I looked down and saw a woman in the water beckoning to me to jump. She had long black hair that cascaded over her sea-shell covered breasts (slightly too small for a D-shell), and an obvious tail. She looked magnificent. "36-22-eighty pence a pound," giggled a voice in my head. I rubbed my eyes and the mermaid vanished. A passing van honked its horn. "Flamin' idiot," shouted the driver. "Get off of there, you damn fool."

Indignant, I swung around to give him the finger, lost my balance and tumbled head first towards the drink.

When I came round I found myself in a small, ornate rowing boat. "Are you OK?" a man was asking. "You're lucky I was there. Do you hurt anywhere? My bags broke your fall. I can drop you off here or row you back over to St Thomas's if you'd prefer. It really isn't a problem."

I knew that voice. Low and hypnotic. I tried to blink him into focus. I was suddenly aware of my back aching, but I wasn't in any great pain.

"Here will do fine, thanks," I said, scrambling to my feet.

"Can you climb that ladder?"

"Yes, I'm OK. Thanks again."

Dazed, I started to clamber up the metal rungs attached to the north side of the Thames embankment.

"Here, you've dropped this," said the man, who stood up and slipped a CD into my jacket pocket.

"Did I?"

"Yes, and these." He placed a small packet of sweets into my hand. Again with the sweets? I looked at my saviour. It was the tramp; the dusky hobo from outside Waterloo East station. In the daylight his skin looked like tooled leather.

"You!" I said. "What, how…?"

"One good turn deserves another."

"But how…"

"No time," said the man, rowing away. "We'll speak again, my boy, of that I'm sure."

I clung to the ladder for a moment. What would a tramp be in a hurry for? And why was he rowing himself about on the Thames anyway? What was going on? Maybe I did need the hospital. Or urgent psychiatric help. I looked back to where the boat should have been but a river bus was passing and by the time it had gone, the tramp and his smaller vessel had vanished. Had he ever been there? He must have been. Otherwise how had I got here, and why wasn't I wet?

I peered to the left and to the right. There was still no sign of the rowing boat. My clothes were dirty, my mouth was dry, and my head felt like it had a corporation dust-cart trapped inside it. But less than a quarter of a mile away, Brian Clarkson would be sitting crying over his useless, charcoaled files. And that thought alone made life worth living.

It was starting to get dark. In an hour or so, the streets would be full of suits and skirts hurling themselves like lemmings into the tubes and railway stations. Rushing, rushing, rushing back to grab an hour or two of sad telly, grunted chat, micro-waved swill and the increasingly infrequent begrudged squelch, before starting the whole dispiriting process all over again the next morning. Hurrying and scurrying, like tiny ants intent on other people's purposes, slaving for someone else from the minute they left school until the moment they drop. It was what I had been doing and what I'd certainly do again. That's life, that's what all the people say...

As I thought the words, I braced myself for a hologram of Sinatra to appear but nothing happened. Maybe the madness was wearing off.

Ahead of me, grey and imposing, stood the Houses of Parliament – an ancient myth kept alive by custom, self-interest and the cynical media. What was it really? Just a rubber stamp for Brussels, just a few hundred cubic feet of hot air and impressive architecture...

Something was happening behind me. A red-faced man of considerable importance, with a considerable girth and a considerable flock of toadies to prove it, had emerged from the Commons. He was so plump and pink that he momentarily morphed into a pig. A sleaze of newspaper hacks surrounded him.

"Anything to tell the public, Minister?" a rat-like reporter asked.

The man's eyes glazed over. "Only," he growled, "that our objectives remain the same and that indeed as has been made clear by the Prime Minister in a speech this morning that our objectives are very clear, and the one about the removal of these extremists is not something we have as a clear objective to implement but it is possible as a consequence, in the mean time it remains imperative that we protect our traditional freedoms with vigour and determination and if the Cabinet decide that the most efficient way to protect them is to temporarily put them on hold in the interests of continued democratic progress and the greater good then so be it. I trust I've made myself clear."

The journalists looked at him blankly as the toadies clapped and cheered. The man swept past them and eased his flabby frame his waiting Jaguar XJ220. "Carlton, Jerry," he grunted. And away they drove into the rush-hour traffic.

Now the press were bored. I slipped them a worried look, my concern was fuelled by the shape-changing that only I could see as faces sprouted whiskers, bodies grew tails, heads expanded, eyes changed colour. A rat pack! And as I stared at them, open-mouthed, so their interest in me began to grow and spread. I didn't like this one bit. Paranoia comes to man too easily. The state I was in, most people would have looked at me twice. But I didn't stop to reason this through. My head still aching, I took to my heels, sprinting over the busy road and down into Westminster tube station. "Mind the gap," said the taped voice as the train pulled in, adding, as the doors closed behind me: "Mind the gap between perception and reality..."

Grabbing the last seat, I sank back and studied the adverts, and then sat straight back up again. The first ad quite clearly bore a picture of my little saviour tramp pal, only in this he was wearing a suit and tie and a Trilby hat. The words said: *'Theo Jinnee, Private Investigator, Seer & Believer, Transcendental Mediation & Massage Service: Mysteries Solved, Wrongs Righted, Wolves Smited, Libidos Restored'.*

It gave an address as the Cosmic Detective Agency, South London branch, and an address in New Cross Road, SE14. I wrote it down on the back of a discarded Metro and got off the tube at Embankment. It was ten past five. I'd get my normal train from Charing Cross but jump off at New Cross. Me and Mr. Jinnee needed to have a chat. As I queued to get off, I noticed a Poem On The Underground series, part of a verse by Ezra Pound: *Towards the Noel that morte saison/(Christ make the shepherds' homage dear!)/Then when the grey wolves everychone/Drink of the winds their chill small-beer...*

As soon as I got to that third line, I heard a distant howling that persisted until I left the train.

Police Car

I walked straight past the panda car parked in Villiers Street, without even noticing it. The two occupants sat locked in silence, lost in private fears and a smog of smouldering resentment and insecurities. Constable Ethan Sneed was slouched in the passenger seat absent-mindedly drumming his fingers on the dashboard in time to a faraway beat. Not long out of Hendon, Sneed was never quite sure that enough was being done. He was a pale tin-ribbed youth not much wider than a lamp post. His earnest, hairless face was a good fifteen inches from forehead to chin, with a red up-turned nose in the centre which was permanently running and which he was permanently wiping with what might once have been a paper tissue. He rarely stopped fidgeting, his lanky body looking forever cramped and uncomfortable, as if it were battling to escape the constraints of his uniform.

In contrast 35 year old Jonathan James Watts was working himself up into a rage in the driver's seat as he read the latest asylum seeker exclusive in the *Daily Express*. It was one of the few things that could be relied on to fire him up these days. Watts had grown slovenly over the years of failed exams, questionable arrests and uninspired adventures. He knew he would never rise about the bottom rung of the Job's career structure. He got by financially, of course, minor corruption saw to that, but Watts was occasionally troubled by sense that he had been dealt a bum hand by his superiors. In his spare time, to relieve his frustration, he wrote long and imaginative poison pen letters to his desk sergeant, a portly Geordie called Eddie Allday who was known in the force as Ethel for reasons no-one could clearly remember – "although he does eff all, all day," Watts often snorted. It was one of the regular laughs to be had in Agar Street Lice Station. (The 'Po' had fallen off years before, but nobody ever bothered to put it up again. Considering the state of Spratt's personal hygiene, it seemed apt.)

Although married and a life-long racist, Watts had become obsessively smitten with the wife of his local curry-house owner, a bi-sexual Anglo-Indian beauty from Bangalore called Minjita. Occasionally Watts would chuck a brick through their windows so he'd have an excuse to speak to her or escort her somewhere "for your own safety, madam."

Sneed looked at his partner. "Didn't there use to be an amusement park near here?" he asked.

"Battersea Fun Fair," Watts grunted.

"Was it any good?"

"Not really," he replied. "Full of pikies. The scariest ride was the night bus home."

Watts spoke with a clipped estuary accent, dripping in deluded superiority. Sneed waited for his partner to say more. He didn't.

"You got any kids, JJ?" Sneed asked nervously, cursing the boyish high pitch of his voice.

Watts looked up from his paper with a sigh. "One, of the male gender," he said wearily.

"Oh yeah, what's he doing then?"

"When last seen he was in bed sleeping. He is, in short, of tender age and modest achievements. He stands roughly eighteen inches high, weights fourteen pounds, and exhibits an alarming tendency to scream out at the slightest inconvenience."

"A proper little nipper, eh?" Sneed ventured, desperately trying to come over like a man of the world. "How does the missus cope?"

"She performs her wifely functions adequately, but if the truth be told no word has passed between us since the night the child was conceived. She gets on with her duties and I get on with mine, eliminating the need for frivolous verbal exchanges. In my house the right to remain silent is more like an obligation. In fact I'd go so far as to say that the only way for men and women to co-exist is to remove verbal communication from the equation. A series of grunts, nods and looks should suffice. If I were your age I'd be looking for a bride from the more northern end of Eastern Europe with no knowledge of the English language whatsoever. Or feminism come to that."

Watts had incredibly thick lips that would curl up and out as he spoke, obscuring much of his nose and chin from view. When he was not speaking they stuck violently together, protruding like a duck's bill. His enemies called his Quackers. As he had no friends, it was a widespread misnomer.

Sneed looked out of the window, feeling out of place. This was nothing like Blue Bloods. Law enforcement was something of a letdown for him. He'd been brought up on the Force. His dad had been a constable for thirty years and had spoon-fed his only son with exaggerated tales of his daring deeds virtually since birth. His home had been a shrine to the Met, littered with Police Gazettes, purloined police equipment, and portraits of famous coppers through the ages, from Robert Peel to Burnside of The Bill via Robert Mark (the latter imaginatively framed in a huge black tyre of the sort he had frequently advocated in 1970s TV adverts). Now retired, the rise of the openly gay Brian Paddick had both revolted and intrigued Sneed Senior for several months. Eventually, after much internal agonising, he had added a framed signed colour photograph of the Met's Deputy Assistant Commissioner to the downstairs toilet, livened up with a fetching pink Versace wrap.

Ethan Sneed had worn his first junior police uniform on a family outing to the coast when he was eight years old. He often recalled the way his father's face had flushed with pride when he'd caught his Uncle Harry 'exposing himself and committing an act of gross indecency' (he was piddling behind a tree) on the way home, and had written down all his particulars in his little black book. What if the old man could see him now? Sneed blushed, embarrassed to be doing nothing. He wished his partner was a proper Old Testament copper looking for eyes for eyes and social workers to punch, but Watts described himself as "a gentleman policeman", and saw his role as "prevention not detention." In practice, this meant that he left the squad car as little as possible preferring to notch up the necessary arrests by the more time-effective methods of planting evidence on people he didn't like the look of.

"This is well boring, Wattsy," said Sneed, finally snapping. "Can't we do some arresting?"

Jon Watts looked at his eager young side-kick and remembered his own novice enthusiasm, back in those heady innocent days when he had actually paid for his own holidays. "Why not, my son, why not?"

***

The beauty of getting on at Charing Cross was the train was sitting there waiting for you and there was easy access to a Cornish pasty stand, The Pasty Shop, which boasted that its produce was 'handmade in Cornwall' as opposed presumably to being machine-tooled in Macclesfield. I rustled up enough change for a steak and Cornish ale pasty and headed for my normal carriage. Disappointingly it was no emptier here than it usually was at Waterloo East. I squeezed into my normal seat, next to the usual delicate 18-stone trainee anorexic who was busy demolishing a pub-sized jar of pickled eggs, absent-mindedly spraying all around her with small flecks of yolk and vinegar. I remembered the CD that the old tramp had given me, rested the pasty on my lap and took it out of my pocket. The cover was weird, just three figures on a dark stairwell. The title was Stairwell To Hell. Not exactly original. I flipped it over. The band name was Indestructible Wolves, which sounded spiky enough. There were thirteen track titles: Clockwork, Inferno, ACAB, You've Been Framed, The Great Escape, Church of Hate, Killer, Sanctuary, Revelation, Dreamland, Delapsus Angelus, Crazy Train, Apo-calypso, Angelic Upstart and Demon Or Godhead. Hmm, so some metal references and some punk. Might be good.

Outside the whistle blew. Right on cue, Biffo burst in shouting down his mobile phone about Millwall and stepping on my foot. He had to stand, and so he proceeded to, with his considerable beer-gut intruding into my personal space. Ah, South East Trains where the speed of a rush-hour bus meets the comfort of the ducking stool.

We set off, but jerked to a halt at the end of the platform. Estuary Man opposite was talking about how his wife had developed tennis elbow – it didn't involve tennis – and my hefty neighbour was making eyes at my pasty. What she really needs, I thought, is a gravy train.

What was the delay this time, then? Had a badger eaten the junction box, had metal thieves nicked the tracks? Maybe there was black ice on the line, or a vestal virgin had been tied down by a cad twirling an unfeasibly bullish moustache. Funny how people never fight on the tops of trains any more, it used to happen all the time in old films.

I tried to eat the pasty quickly without making too much mess. It was only when I started to push a few crumbs under the seat with my foot that I spotted a familiar face on the front of the *Evening Standard* which Estuary Man was reading. It was ME!

The headline screamed 'Wanted!' followed in smaller but hysterical 50point type: 'Cops hunt the Arson Fugitive.' Arson Fugitive? Cops? Oh lumme. Feelings of fear, combined with guilt, consumed me, resulting naturally in an entirely rational surge of paranoia. The dude with the headphones was giving me the stink eye, even the chipmunk secretaries seemed to be glowering in my direction. They looked like cute Disney characters re-drawn by Frank Miller. Sweat broke out on my temples. It was then that Estuary Man caught my knee with his foot; I panicked and did what any other hapless teenager would do in the circumstances. I bolted. Out of my seat, out of the train, down the platform, over the barriers and back out into the West End.

"Go on my son!" hollered Biffo.

"He must be on a promise," Estuary Man sniggered. The fat woman smirked and helped herself to the remains of my pasty.

***

In Villiers Street, the two cops were getting excited. "So where shall we start?" asked Sneed.

"First we find a suspect, anyone suspicious-looking about?" Watts smiled inwardly. Racial epithets had become the kiss of career death in the Met, but here in the freedom of his panda car,

Watt could and did employ them with relish. "Any sign of blacks, Paks, pikeys, poofs, kikes, Albanians…"

"No." Sneed groaned inwardly. Watts didn't have minor peeves; he had major sociopathic issues…

"Students, scroungers, right-wingers, left-wingers, Goths, gypoes, dippers, drippers, asylum seekers, squeegee merchants, squatters, skate-boarders, skinheads, punks…"

"No."

"Turks, truants, Frogs, thickoes, chavs, crusties, Hell's Angels, hooligans, unemployed layabouts…"

"Nope."

"How about window cleaners? They're generally of a criminal bent, I find. A God-send to the poor constable endeavouring to meet his quota. Or eyeties, Taffs, Nips, tiddlies, queers, or any other species of lowlife that I may have so far omitted…"

"There is one swarthy looking bloke over by the park. He's been there about five minutes."

"Loitering with intent, eh?"

"Actually, he was watching the pigeons."

Watts's weasel eyes lit up. "A rare and unnatural pursuit if you ask me, young Sneed, reeking of criminal possibilities."

"But he was feeding them crusts of bread."

"Well, that puts the proverbial tin hat on it, my son. Come with me lad and allow me to demonstrate the finer technicalities of the law enforcement process."

Watts turned the ignition and started to drive the few yards to Victoria Embankment Gardens. As he approached the entrance, a fast moving object collided with the car bonnet. It was me. As my limp body somersaulted into the air, the officers grinned at each other.

"Blimey," smiled Sneed. "He's five foot off the ground."

"Then he is guilty of leaving the scene of a crime – to wit, damaging police property – and must be taken into custody post haste," Watts decided.

"And he was obstructing the police," Sneed added jubilantly, feeling part of the team for the first time. Oh this was going to be good.

***

Well that hurt. I was flat out on the road, but there were no bones broken. I opened my eyes to see a fat police sergeant looming over me.

"Practising for the next Olympics are we sir?" Watts asked, his nasally voice soaked in vinegary sarcasm.

I didn't have the energy to reply.

"You've given Constable Sneed here a very nasty turn, viciously attacking police property like that. Come on, what's the moniker, sunshine?"

I looked at him blankly, I was dazed, confused and exhausted.

"Monica Sunshine?" I stuttered. "Sorry, officer, I don't know her."

"Don't give us lip, arse-hole," snapped Sneed, the redness of his nose exploding over the entire length of his long angular face. "What's your bleedin' name?"

"Oh sorry. Scrimshaw. Thomas Scrimshaw."

"Are you taking the piss?"

"No, no, that's my name. Thomas Scrimshaw. I'm an office worker."

"Where do you work?" asked Sneed.

"I work, well I used to work, well until today I was at..." I hesitated, deciding against telling them the drama of the afternoon.

"Well are you working or did you used to work?" said Watts, with a deathly smirk. "From where I'm standing you barely look fit to be standing on a Streatham street corner selling the Big Issue. What kind of a tool goes to an office dressed like that? Your clothes are a mess, your shoes are filthy and your hair is all over the place. You're a state man, a disgrace. What does he look like Sneed?"

"Like he's been pulled through Jo Brand's granny's fanny backwards."

"Yes indeed," said Watts, his bestial lips curling with distaste. "And congratulations on that lovely turn of phrase. This bears further investigation, indeed it does. Get in the car!"

"Oh yes," Sneed babbled excitedly. "Oh, yes-yes-yes-yes-yes."

Thomas Scrimshaw Is In A Cell, OK?

Day Eight. I was no longer fully asleep, but neither was I in any hurry to wake up. I'd had a bad night on a hard, unfamiliar bed. In a cell! I had spent the night in a police cell. At least it would impress Matty.

The cell was Dickensian in its simplicity. Apart from the wooden bed and an old-fashioned chamber pot it was completely empty. There was no TV or radio. The once white walls were blitzed with graffiti, a spiralling mess of bad language ('Fuck the system', 'Revolution Now!'), defiance ('ACAB'), warnings ('Watch your back!'), repentance ('Sorry, Mum'), self-pity, vulgar sexual drawings, vile racism and the occasional joke ('Trap door this way' with an arrow pointing down). I added 'Thomas, Nemesis' with my thumbnail.

My dreams, such as they were, remained as baffling as Klingon algebra: all my friends had been involved along with Ozzy, Brian Clarkson, New Cross station (again), the Kaiser Chiefs repeatedly singing "Oh my God I can't believe it, never been this far away from home"...and David Letterman and Jay Leno appeared to talking about me on a giant TV screen, but when I'd tried to turn up the volume, the knob came off in my hand. The girls had been there too, Kez, and Freeje, even Natalie from the Lantern but my knob didn't come off in their hands because they were too busy fighting each other. And then the distant wolf started baying. And everyone started running, except for me; I'd just opened an exit door and stepped into a strange colourful arena with flashing lights, a cacophony of clicks, whirs and other odd background noises and hundreds of leather-clad spectators cheering as a strange thunderous whooshing sound grew louder in the background...until I woke up. Weird and weirder.

"Don't worry Thomas; everything will work itself out my friend."

"Who's there?"

I strained his eyes against the darkness. It was nearly dawn. The man was mopping the cell floor.

"This is a strange time for cleaning," I said weakly.

"Time is going to get a whole lot stranger..." he laughed. "Trust me, you won't regret this. These are things you have to go through before you can experience the real truth, the deeper truth, the Secrets, the Great Reason..."

"Jimmy!"

Another voice, but this one came from outside the cell.

"You're the tramp again, aren't you," I said.

"Well I prefer the term, gentleman of the road, but yes. Tis I."

"And your name is Jimmy?"

"People call me that."

"But your advert says you're called Theo Jinnee..."

"Jimmy/Jinnee, what's a couple of consonants between friends?"

The tramp laughed again which made me angry, but then I looked at the man's face in the half light and he appeared to be aging in front of my eyes. His body was almost translucent, and his face was now lined as deeply as a corduroy cap.

"To find yourself you must find me," he said. Then his features began to quiver. For a moment he was there, vibrating, then he vanished. Jimmy/Jinnee had gone.

"NO!" I screamed. "NO!" I must have finally flipped. I didn't get to think about it too long however as another face appeared. It was lupine and hairy and it belonged to a man with deep, coal-black eyes full of hatred who said simply "I am coming. Your arse is mine, boy..."

The soiled plaster walls of the cell became lighter and started to spin. Then darkness clouded my brain.

ACAB – All Coppers Are…

MY body was an hour glass. Slowly the sleep drained out ⸗ leaving only the cold emptiness of a new day, and the fear. I was up to my neck in something I couldn't explain and I didn't like it one bit. In my calmer moments I'd managed to convince myself that I would get through this ordeal unscathed. After all, all of the charges – the fire, the "assault" on the police car – were clearly accidents. As for the Jinnee's disappearance and the nasty guy's brief appearance, I concluded they must have been part of the bizarre Leno/Letterman dream. Nothing to fret about. I'd be fine.

I got out of bed, stepped on the mop he'd left behind, and fell right back down again in a shock. Just then, the cell door opened and a small, elderly gentleman, dressed immaculately in a smart three-piece Prince of Wales checked suit, came in. He twitched nervously, like a rabbit, and his manner of talking, as if nibbling at his words before timidly spitting them out while his nostrils contracted and expanded, underlined this hare-y impression.

"G-g-good morning, er, Mr Scrimshaw," he said nervously. "Newman is the name. George Frederick Henry Newman. I'm to act in your defence."

"Defence for what?" I snapped. "I've done nothing."

"Oh dear, I was hoping you weren't going to be in any trouble. I was rather hoping you would plead guilty and save the authorities any bother."

"Look, what have I been accused of, because I swear to you I'm as innocent as the day is long."

Newman looked hurt. "Now, now, please, none of that. You know full well you've committed a number of heinous crimes, some of them quite shocking in their severity. Please be reasonable for your own good. If you plead guilty you'll get a light sentence, say nine or ten years. But if you plead not guilty, when you are convicted they'll throw away the key."

I stepped towards him, angry again. "Why should I plead guilty when I'm innocent? What shocking crimes am I supposed to have committed? And you're supposed to be a defence lawyer...you look like you'd have trouble convincing a jury that Big Ben is a clock tower."

Newman twitched wildly. "Oh, you're a perfect wretch," he seethed, cupping his little hands together in rage. "Mr. Watts," he shouted. "I've tried to reason with him." Watts and Sneed burst in. "But he's an obstinate beast. Perhaps you and your colleague can make him see sense. Newman left the two cops to their devices.

They made me wear a hood and stand in the stress position – spread-eagled, legs apart, my back arched inwards, and my fingertips against the cell wall. It hurt like buggery. If I rested my head against the wall, a hand slammed my face against it. If I put my palms against it, I was slapped. When I fell, they punched and booted me back to my feet. Inside the hood I could not tell which direction the blows were coming from or where they were aimed at. This went on until I passed out. But there was no peace even when I slept, because in my dreams I was visited by an angry wolf who transformed into the hairy, aggressive man who'd threatened me before. "I am coming for you Scrimshaw," the man-wolf snarled every time. "And there is no escape. No escape! Your arse is mine." Again with the arse, is all I remember thinking.

The Trial

Day Twelve. Day followed night followed day. Sometimes I went without food, sometimes water. My interrogations came randomly but were always the same. The same blinding lights in my face, the same questions endlessly repeated, the same absurd accusations hurled at me with the conviction of religious zealots. I felt like I was lost in a fog. Until the morning Watts and Sneed turned up smiling.

"Make yourself pretty, sunshine, today's your big day," Watts chortled. One a side, they marched me down a corridor that seemed to go on forever. The policemen didn't speak and there was no-one else in sight. The lights appeared to get brighter as we went, and their footsteps louder, but I could still hear his own heart beating like a bass drum b – boom, boom, BOOM! I felt like I was going to explode.

They stopped in front of two massive double doors about ten feet high and made of solid oak. There was an inscription carved in the wall above them: 'Mundus vult decipi, ergo decipiatur'. And to the side 'Justicia est constupro' with 'Monstra mihi pecuniam' and 'Pecunia non olet' written below it. I concentrated hard but couldn't work out the meaning. My Latin was too rusty.

"Don't worry," Watts said conspiratorially. "The last chap who was here with the same charges got a suspended sentence."

"Really?"

"Yeah, they hanged him." Ha, bloody ha.

"Here wear this," said Sneed, handing me a blindfold.

"What? Why?"

"Just put it on," snapped Watts.

I did as I was told, then Sneed slipped a hangman's noose loosely around my neck and knocked on the door of the court.

I heard the door open. "Whom have you there?" a man asked solemnly.

"Mr. Thomas Scrimshaw, a poor sinner in a state of darkness," answered Watts. "He comes of his own free will and accord, properly prepared, humbly soliciting to be admitted to the mysteries and privileges of English justice."

"I don't..." I started to say.

"Shut it!" commanded Sneed.

Watts pulled my shirt open and the court official held a dagger to my left breast, teasing the flesh with the point.

"Do you feel anything?" he asked.

"Ow, yes."

"Enter Thomas Scrimshaw."

Watts and Sneed took an arm each and led me into what turned out to be the courtroom to the sound of hissing and booing. I was led twenty paces forward, up some stairs and left standing.

"All rise for Lord Justice Crack," said a voice. The commotion stopped as everyone in the court got to their feet as Francis Algernon Peregrine Crack entered.

"Mr Scrimshaw, remove your blindfold." The same voice.

I did so. The court was heaving.

"The prisoner is in the dock, M'Lud."

I looked at the Judge. He was an old man, he could have been ninety; he could in fairness have been 190. His face was fierce and his white hair was closely shorn in the Prussian military style. Crack's skin was pale, his lips thin. He wore old-fashioned, black and thick-rimmed bank manager's spectacles over a beaked nose. He looked like a painting from a haunted house that had come to life.

Around the bench directly in front of him, sat a number of grim-faced men, peering at me like hungry vultures over their thick ledgers. Had I been any closer to them, I would have noticed cobwebs and heavy layers of dust in the crevices of their faces. I shivered. I glanced around the court room and was met with a row of hostile eyes. The jury. I looked away and whispered a prayer to the god I still did not believe in.

A familiar odour wafted over, musty and oppressive. Files. I smelt files. Turning back, I spotted Clarkson in the pilchard-packed public gallery, his chin pushing out like Mussolini. Oh and surprise, surprise, with the inevitability of dry rot, Miss Simms had turned up too.

She was sitting glumly between Clarkson and what looked like Iggy Pop's grandad but was actually Dugash. Behind them was Mum looking worried, and a scowling Frank, and over to the side my friends Matt, Mark and Keziah.

My defence barrister Mr Newman, the Rabbit Man, was sitting just a few feet to my left, nibbling at his fingernails. On the opposite side of the same aisle was a lean, austere looking man with a wolfish smile, who seemed to be growling at Newman. He was the man-wolf from my nightmares. His name, I would soon learn, was the Prosecutor, Stannard von Wolfson.

"Sit," commanded the Judge.

Wolfie rose to his feet. "Your honour, the accused is charged with premeditated arson," he rasped. "It is the Crown's case that he did knowingly set fire to a number of valuable and irreplaceable files belonging to the Authority" (the courtroom gasped, Clarkson nodded seriously). "He is also accused of sedition, conspiracy, supply and use of class A narcotics (a huge boo), assault, obstructing the police, damaging police property" (again the courtroom showed its disapproval), "and trying to get some enjoyment out of life." (People were shouting "shame, shame" and a man in the gallery yelled "Hang the bastard!").

The Judge looked at me and sneered.

"How does he plead?" he asked Newman.

"Not guilty, your honour."

"Not what?"

"Guilty."

"That's better." The Judge began to writing. "Guilty..., there. So I sentence you..."

Wolfie looked alarmed. "The press, your worship, the press," he hissed quickly.

I was horrified. Was this England? I leapt to my feet. "Hold on," I hollered, my anger momentarily overcoming my fear. "I don't recognise this court."

"That's because it's been redecorated," Watts wise-cracked behind me.

"Silence!" snapped the judge. "Now again, how does your client plead?" he asked the Rabbit Man.

"Not guilty," he said in a whisper.

"Not what?"

"He pleads not guilty, your honour."

"Oh very well."

"If I may crave the court's indulgence," the Rabbit Man said. "I would like to request an adjournment until the prison psychiatrist has had time to furnish his report, clearly the evidence is so over-whelming that a not guilty plea is bordering on absurd. I suspect the report will justify a plea of guilty but insane."

I looked on blankly. This was the defence?

The judge looked at Bunny Boy with ill-disguised hostility. "I am sure you will find this court reasonably indulgent as the trial progresses, Mr Newman," he said with a sneer. "But don't set out by trying its patience. Unnecessary delays in criminal trials cost money and are an unwanted burden for the tax-payer, something I'm sure you will both bear in mind by keeping witnesses and verbosity to a minimum. Mr von Wolfson, you may proceed with the prosecution case."

The Wolf Man rose and began to speak – if that's the right word – very passionately. Try as I may, I couldn't make out a single word he said, yet it must have been very good indeed because the public gallery had erupted with cheers. As their yells of encouragement increased, so did the intensity of the Prosecutor's speech. I heard something about messages. Baring his yellow teeth and licking his lips, Wolfie held aloft several sheets of emails taken from my computers at home and at work and print-outs of WhatsApp texts. His body seemed to increase in size in correspondence to his mounting passion as, nostrils aquiver, he read them out. By the time he reached "Exhibit 13" - the one that said 'I shda torched the fat toad' - the nostrils were opening and closing at an alarming rate, so much so that they were little more that a blur in the centre of his face. His hands were everywhere. Suddenly Clarkson was on his feet too, waving his walrus fists in agreement. Feeding off this support physically and vocally, Wolfie swelled up for his climax.

Then, just at the noise was becoming unbearable, the Prosecutor finished and collapsed, huddling into a tiny ball on the floor of the court, twitching and snarling.

When the applause had died down, Newman, the little Rabbit Man, got up to speak. Immediately the Prosecutor was on his feet again, snarling at him. Newman gave a small start and sat down straight away, quaking in his seat. Satisfied, von Wolfson sat down again too and started to lick himself like a dog, revelling in the salty taste of his own body.

Astonished, I rose slowly to my feet and began to explain just how the grinding monotony of my work had driven me to the sanctity of the Gents and how Clarkson's attitude had then driven me to the store room. I explained that the texts had been in jest; I'd wanted to work, of course I had, but that I needed some fulfilment out of a job. I wanted my life to have a point. Against a sonic wall of jeers and cat-calls, I pleaded with the Judge to have mercy on me.

The clerk of the court, Doris Yates shuddered. How could she be expected to write that sort of subversive filth down? A précis; that was the answer. 'The accused rose to his feet and pleaded 'Guilty with mitigating circumstances','" she wrote in her precise shorthand.

All eyes were on the Judge. Five minutes passed. The Judge neither knew nor cared. His eyes were fixed, as they had been for the last half hour, on the shapely body of Lucy Porter in the latest issue of Zoo magazine as he wondered how long it would take to cover every inch of her in maple syrup and then lick it off. He poked his tongue out slightly as he contemplated the matter, which was slightly disconcerting for anyone watching him.

Crack was one of Britain's most famous and powerful judges, renowned for his wisdom, his influence and his baffling inconsistencies. Truly it was said that wherever there was honi soit, his Lordship would be mal y poncing. Born in 1933, he was christened Major-General Frank Crack by the Archbishop of York; his family owned half of Berkshire, which may or may not explain why the *Daily Mirror* had once nicknamed him "the berk of all Berks".

Eventually a bold usher passed him a note asking him to sum up. Unperturbed, Crack removed his notebook, wherein he had written his verdict before breakfast. He cleared his throat. This had to be good, the papers were in.

"In asking the Jury to consider their verdict," he began, "I remind them that what this base criminal has committed is not a mere act of mindless vandalism but one of premeditated political conspiracy…"

"WHAT?!?" I was on my feet shouting.

"SILENCE!" the Judge roared, clutching his ornate gavel in his mottled, arthritic hands and banging it feebly. Truly the best of his class had perished in the Great War. Crack didn't like being interrupted, but I was bobbing up and down like an unexploded mine at high tide. He sighed. He'd have to take me on.

"Mr Scrimshaw," he said patronisingly. "Did you consciously loiter in the lavatories?"

"Well, yeah, but..."

"So you admit you deliberately evaded your responsibilities as an employee."

"I suppose..."

"And thus you were flagrantly flouting Mr Clarkson's authority."

"That old walrus..."

"Mr Scrimshaw," the Judge creaked contemptuously, "'That old walrus' as you so charmingly put it is not only a well respected figure, but he is also *in loco society*. By flouting his authority, you are showing your criminal disrespect for the moral values of civilised society at large. You are in contempt of court, of the Crown and Government itself. You, you, ah…"

I sank back into my seat while the Judge fumbled for his notes.

"Ah yes, Scrimshaw's actions," he quoted, "in attempting to shirk his responsibilities led him to serious criminal conclusions. In deliberately setting fire to the Authority's filing system he is guilty not only of arson, but more seriously of sedition and terrorism. Scrimshaw seems to have forgotten that freedom from the grind has to be earned or inherited by those whom by virtue of birth and education have a natural right to them. My God, if everyone acted like he had done the entire structure of our society would be destroyed. We'd be left with anarchy and chaos. Let the Jury bear this in mind when considering their verdict."

At these words, a man dressed as a wrestling referee jogged up to the Jury box and announced: "Now, I want a good clean bout, no biting or scratching, two falls or one submission to find that lovely 'guilty' verdict. Off you go." He blew a whistle and the Jury withdrew. They had clearly been drinking. Some had to be carried out, one was sick on the floor and a large man in a kiss-me-quick hat unzipped his flies and sprayed Newman with steaming urine on the way.

"Take the prisoner back to the cells," the Judge instructed. As I was led off, he smiled and returned to luscious Lucy. The summing up had gone very well. This one, he was certain, would make the front page of the Telegraph. Crack enjoyed being a Judge. In his stunningly undistinguished career he'd only ever committed one crime as one – sexual harassment. Fortunately he'd come up before his brother who after a thoroughly impartial hearing had let off with a caution. His victim, 38 year old nun Brenda Coyle was less lucky. She was sentenced to five months imprisonment on grounds of contributory negligence.

The Jury never returned. Instead, Crack slipped Doris Yates a double-headed coin and asked her to toss it for him. "Heads he's guilty," he said, and then feigned surprise at the verdict.

I was brought back up to find the court awash with smiling faces. Maybe I'd been cleared. I dug a thumbnail into a finger as the jury filed back in.

"Who is the foreman of the jury?" asked the clerk.

"I am," said a familiar voice.

I looked up. Brian Clarkson was now in the jury box, along with Miss Simms, Sneed, Watts and a number of people in party hats who he had never seen before. I looked at Newman who hid his face in his hands. Franz Kafka had nothing on this.

It was so unfair I choked back tears. What a travesty, what a farce. My life and my future were being flushed down the kharzi in front of my eyes. If there was a God then He had truly forsaken me.

I felt vomit rise in my throat and fought it back. I couldn't let the Walrus see he'd beaten me, even though he had. What could I do? The dice had been loaded from the start.

The clerk of the court spoke again. "Have you reached a verdict in respect of each of the charges?"

"We have," Clarkson replied.

"Count one charges Thomas Scrimshaw with premeditated arson," the clerk said. "How do you find him, guilty or not guilty?"

"Guilty," said Clarkson.

"Count two charges Thomas Scrimshaw with damaging police property. How do you find him, guilty or not guilty?"

"Guilty."

"Count three charges Thomas Scrimshaw with leaving the scene of an accident. How do you find him, guilty or not guilty?"

"Guilty."

I began to switch off. Every charge read out – conspiracy, assault, sedition, various terrorist acts, spying for Islamic State, and public disorder at Dale Farm – was greeted with a guilty. The final charge was one of "attempting to get some enjoyment out of life."

"Guilty, guilty, guilty!" said Clarkson triumphantly.

"You bastards!" shouted my Mum, which was surprising.

"Officers, take that woman to the cells," snapped Justice Crack, adding lasciviously "I shall see her in my chambers later."

He turned to Clarkson. "Thank you, Mr. Foreman," he said. "I can't thank you enough. You have done your job well.

"Mr. Scrimshaw. You have been found guilty on all eighteen counts, and rightly too in my opinion. I understand that this is a first offence but in times like these when we are under attack from an enemy within society must take a dim view of all who challenge its conventions. Yours is a shocking case, one of the worst I've heard in over seventy-five years on the bench. Therefore I have no hesitation in sentencing you to ten years imprisonment with a recommendation that you serve a minimum of fifteen. Take him away."

Eh? Did that even make sense? Two court ushers stepped forward and marched me back down towards the cells. I didn't speak. I was having trouble taking it all in. Suddenly they changed direction and took me through a door that I hadn't been through before. Stairs. The stairwell was dark. Dirty. Damp. It stunk like the men's room in an Egyptian brothel, if they had any. Probably piddle out the window on the wallahs below. There's a thought – if the Arabs could have Harrods maybe I could move to Middle East merchandising. Mosque Brothers. Yeah, that had a ring to it. Maybe one day...Maybe one day I'd stop day-dreaming...

I strained my tired peepers against the all-pervading gloom, but couldn't see more that a yard in front of me. It was getting danker with every step we took and the pong was getting on my pips. It smelt like they had incontinent rats down here, as well as on the bench.

In the distance down below I swore I could hear the steady flow of a river. Maybe there was a sewer down here.

The ushers were still clutching my arms, their heavy fingers sinking into my soft flesh. At least they seemed to know where they were going.

"If you two get any closer I'll have to marry one of you," I joked.

"Careful, tosser," the left-hand usher sneered in a voice heavy with catarrh. "We could always say you fell down the stairs trying to get away. And it's a long way down."

The ushers looked like the twin cheeks of one horrendous arse. The men might have been small fish in a very big pool, but they prided themselves on being piranhas. They clung so close as we trekked further into the cold below that it seemed that they were an extension of me. When I moved, they moved. When I breathed, they breathed. Presenting Thomas, the three-headed convict from suburban hell! I'd make a killing in a circus side-show.

For some reason an old rugby song popped into my head: *'The sexual life of a camel is stranger than anyone thinks/At the height of the mating season, he tries to bugger the Sphinx/But the Sphinx's posterior passage is blocked by the sands of the Nile/which accounts for the hump on the camel/And the Sphinx's inscrutable smile..."*

I smiled. I always bloody smiled.

"The boat man will be waiting," the right-hand usher said. Or had they both said it? I glanced from one to the other, but there was no telling which stony-faced son-of-a-bum had spoken.

"Boat man? What are you on about?" I yelped. "Where in God's name are you taking me?"

"Nowhere...in God's name." Both had spoken that time. "You heard the Judge."

"Yeah, but all he said was ten years."

"Fifteen, sucker," the stereophonic answer rang back. "Fifteen years of darkness, fifteen deep dirty years. Bad luck, scum."

"Yeah?" I said defiantly. "We'll see what the European Court of Human Rights has to say about this."

Both men laughed. "Human!" chortled the one on the left.

"Doesn't this," the right-hand usher continued alone. "All seem rather Stygian?"

"Tip-toe down to Pluto," roared the left-hand usher, shaking with laughter. "Down to Pluto, in the dark you'll be. Oh tip-toe down to Hades with me!"

I snapped. "You no-good bastards!" I pulled, kicked and strained against their grip. No use, the fingers just dug deeper. What would Jack Bauer do? Fight back of course. I looked at my tormenters for anything on them I could use to get away, maybe a photo ID pass. It was then I noticed that they both had guns in side holsters. They re-applied their fingers and I shrivelled up, a ball of pain. They were going on about Miktec, Asiutl and Azrael whoever they were. I caught the words "Our Lady" and "Holy Death" but couldn't make any sense of it. I hurt too much. My legs were off the ground, wrapped around my head like boneless tentacles. The agony didn't stop. I needed a picture to fade in to, to lose myself in, to find sanctuary...sanctuary from the law...ah Maiden again...hold on, what about the CD old Jimmy/Jinnee had given me? I managed to reach inside my pocket and pull it out, staring intently at the cover. Yes, it was working. I felt myself being sucked in, only to emerge in the exact same place on the self same stairs with the same two creeps holding on to me. Oh shit. The album cover shot was of US on the stairwell to hell...it wasn't fair, it wasn't right, it was all no use, no use at all. Consciousness started to slip away...

"That'll do." A woman's voice, spoke quietly but with authority. "Slowly now. Let the nice gentleman go."

The ushers turned with their sneers unzipped, but there was no disputing the deadly reality of the small revolver the strikingly beautiful woman clutched in her right hand.

It was her. Freeje, dressed like a rock n roll geisha, with a faint glow of white light around her head. She looked like she'd stepped straight out of a Japanese manga comic. I blinked. Her? Here? How? Why? When? What?

She pulled me away from the ushers. "Here, meet me at this address as soon as," she commanded, slipping me a piece of paper. "Now get your ass out of here."

I didn't need telling twice. I spun round and hurtled back up the stairs, not even flinching as three shots sounded out in darkness. I didn't know that Freeje had shot out the lamp and the ushers had managed to shoot each other as she had made a graceful get-away.

The first shards of light told me I was nearing the courtroom again so I slowed down to a trot, fear welling up inside me.

When I reached the top, I gasped. An orgy was raging. Why did orgies rage by the way? Shouldn't they be happy? And wouldn't you be angrier if there was one going on that you hadn't been invited to? Whatever…

The courtroom was awash in a sea of human flesh. To my right, partly clothed court orderlies were straddling trouser-less coppers, a-moaning and a-groaning and calling out strange words of lust. Watts was in a corner drinking brandy from a hip flask. I bent down and picked some loose coins off the floor, turning my shoulder to shield my face but the cop took no notice of me. A woman had sashayed up to Watts, unbuttoning her blouse. She smelt of nicotine and Baileys. "You have the right to remain naked, my dear," he chortled, as he ripped off his shirt and the two of them joined the flabby, heaving hordes.

I walked on. To my left was the jury box filled with drunken, beer-swilling men who were playing darts and yelling "180" and "Cocky on the oche" repeatedly, amid great blasts of spit-speckled laughter. Two court orderlies had stripped off and were sharing a crack pipe. Everywhere else there were pink and paunchy couples copulating and naked people drinking.

To avoid suspicion, I slipped out of my clothes, rolled them into a bundle and started walking very calmly to the doors. I tried to keep cool by concentrating on the dullest most sexless thing I could think of – ITV's Loose Women – but to no avail. Two yards into the throbbing, shuddering mass of love-making and I realised my favourite feature was standing up like a flagpole.

"What's the hurry, honey?" a young Sienna Miller look-alike purred. "It's obvious you don't want to leave. In fact it stands out a mile."

"I, erh…"

"I'm Lucy, and I'd love to suck your lollipop…" She smiled so seductively I almost orgasmed on the spot. What to do? She was drop-dead gorgeous, and she'd just dropped to her knees. I was looking a gift gobble in the mouth but I didn't know her from Victoria Adams and, more important than my own sense of morality, I only had a limited amount of time to escape from this horny hell-hole. Beautiful blonde Lucy grabbed my manhood and pulled me towards her. The upstanding member was more than happy to lay back and think of England, but at that critical moment I spotted Judge Crack wearing a pince-nez. Cross-eyed with lust, his Lordship was taking a 14 stone lady juror from behind while drooling over a photograph of a schoolboy that was attached to her back with gaffa tape. Beyond him, von Wolfson had morphed into a three-dimensional cartoon werewolf and was chasing a human-sized rabbit around the courtroom. This was too weird and way too risky.

"What's up?" asked Lucy.

"Sorry I've gotta go," I answered, reluctantly easing her aside.

"What are you, some kind of faggot?" she snapped.

"Sorry," I smiled. "Another time? Maybe? Please? It'd be nice to get to know you first…"

I pressed on through the thrusting, lusting throng, hastily slipping my shirt back on.

"It's him!" she screamed. "It's Scrimbo!" (Scrimbo?!) "He's getting away." No-one took a blind bit of notice. If it makes it any easier, I thought, it meant something to me, oh Sienna.

***

Matt, Mark, and Keziah had left the court room as soon as Thomas had been sentenced and were drowning their sorrows in the near-by Pig & Wig pub (established 1812, ruined 1993).

"The Standard is calling that idiot judge 'the Law's prime asset'," snorted Mark.

"I think the 'et' is silent," Matt replied.

"He will be OK, won't he?" Keziah asked for only the fifth time.

"Course he will, Kez," said Matt. "The trial was joke."

"He must have more grounds for appeal than the Bridgewater Three," added Mark.

"Who?" asked Keziah.

"Those people who got put away for murdering a paper boy," Mark explained.

"Yeah," said Matt. "Down in Devon. Simon and Garfunkel wrote a song about it, Trouble Over Bridgewater."

"No, it was up in the Midlands somewhere, and the kid's name was Bridgewater," Mark corrected him. "The Old Bill faked the confessions, I think. Simon and Garfunkel were the defence lawyers."

"Will you all just stop joking for once?" Keziah snapped. "This isn't funny. Poor Tom."

"He'll be OK, Kez," said Matt. "He'll appeal."

"How long did it take the Bridgewater people to appeal?" she asked.

"Eighteen years," replied Mark, now sounding worried.

"It might not be that easy," said Matt. "Look." He pointed at the pub TV. There was a picture of Thomas on screen.

"Turn it up, mate," he implored the bored barman who sighed and complied.

ITN news reader Mark Austin looked as solemn as a pall-bearer. "We interrupt this programme for an important newsflash," he said. "The Metropolitan Police today issued an appeal for help from the public after a dangerous sociopath escaped from custody."

The director cut to a picture of Thomas which had been reddened and tampered with to give the impression of slight horns. It was captioned 'Scrimbo'. "Two court ushers were wounded when Thomas 'Scrimbo' Scrimshaw staged an audacious break-out aided by members of a terrorist cell.

Scrimshaw, 17, an anarchist, was earlier sentenced to fifteen years for arson and subversion. He is described as armed and dangerous. Security at ports and airports has been placed on full alert. Anyone seeing this man is advised not to attempt to apprehend him but to contact the authorities immediately. Now we return to Make Me Perfect..."

The screen was immediately filled by a fat topless woman on an operating table who was being enthusiastically sliced open by a man in a butcher's coat. Nip/Yuck. The barman clicked off the sound.

"Armed and dangerous?" said Keziah, puzzled.

"Who could have sprung him?" whispered Matt.

"People like him want stringing up," said the barman loudly. "Bloody anarchists. Probably one of yer Taliban mob. I'd hang the bleedin' lot of 'em; it's the only language they understand."

"They're more likely speak Pashto," muttered Kez under her breath. Mark sushed her.

"Any more drinks here, gents?"

"Not for us thanks mate," said Matt. "We've got to get home. We're expecting a friend."

Book Two: Roads to Nowhere

Prologue II

Day 27. *I suppose now would be a good time to find God, hurtling up through the stratosphere, without a ship, wondering how I'm still breathing and how many of my mates might not be.*

I never set out to be a hero, much less a super one. Yet here I am with the fate of the world resting on my shoulders. Yeah, my shoulders, when I can barely be trusted to change a fuse.

Come on God, come through for me.

I was seventeen when all this started, and to tell you the truth the only Great Unknown on my mind was girls. At this point, I hadn't become Public Enemy Number One. I hadn't been tormented by my own nightmares. I hadn't been on trial for a murder I hadn't committed. I wasn't even aware of my guardian angel the Jinnee, the self-styled "Master of the Macabre" and by far the most powerful Magus ever to cast himself as the humble servant of humankind.

If you'd told me then I was about to spend most of my time dicing with death I'd have probably cracked some rotten joke about cutting carrots with Pluto or playing craps with a funeral director. I'll warn you now my gags won't get any better. I'm Tom by the way; Thomas to my Mum, Tommy to my Dad and something fairly unprintable to my stepdad Frank the plank.

I've grown up a lot over the last few weeks. I've had to.

Mum always says I have a lucky face. And I suppose I have...compared to the rest of me at any rate.

I'm still rising fast, shooting up through the thermosphere. If I'd known I was going to be travelling this far, I'd have brought a change of underwear. I certainly need one.

Why wasn't the cold killing me, by the way? Was this proof that the Almighty was doing his bit for me? Maybe it would help if I'd believed in Him in the first place...Maybe I should try praying to Zeus instead. Or was that like a hypochondriac asking for a placebo?

Even if I survive this, and I know I'm supposed to, the biggest battle lies ahead for me - the final showdown with Fenrir which, it is written, will decide the fate of our species for the next thousand years. Who wrote it and where I couldn't tell you. But I'm getting ahead of myself. All you need to know right now is that none of this has been my doing. There was never any big Faustian pact involved. I wasn't remotely aware of the changes that were going on within me, and I still don't know why it happened...

Philosophy? Don't Get Me Sartre'd

Day 13. I looked at Freeje's note for the fifteenth time. It still said '22 Lupino Lane xxx.' Three kisses. Oh yeah. But Lupino Lane? It sounded like something out of The Mighty Boosh. If only the gang were here. If only I could contact them. Borrow a mobile maybe, text Kez the address...no, too risky. The cops would probably be monitoring all their phones. No, first things first. I had to find Jimmy or Jinnee or whatever he was calling himself today. He was clearly the key to all this. And that meant staying free...

I'd managed to walk to the Elephant and Castle in Southwark, keeping my head down. The trains were too risky, too exposed. It'd be easier to slip onto a bus. I'd been at this bus stop since 3am, and now the winter sun was peeling away the darkness. There were about fifteen people behind me, possibly as many as twenty. I didn't like to look too closely, didn't want to draw attention to myself. The last few weeks had left me scared and paranoid. I didn't believe in fate or karma but I had a strange growing feeling that something big, something major, something almost certainly malign was coming for me.

On one level, it was probably irrational. Most bad things are the result of cock-ups rather than conspiracies, yet it also seemed entirely possible that someone or some sinister force was after me, but who? M15, the CIA, Mossad, Britain's Got Talent…it could be any of them, it could be all of them. And if I knew the who I still had to figure out the why…

Wearily, I checked my pockets. All I had was the handful of coins I'd found on the court room floor, my Oyster card, Jimmy-Jinnee's sweets and the CD he'd given me. Maybe I'd died. Maybe this was purgatory. Or maybe I was trapped in my own my subconscious like Sam Tyler in Life On Mars. In which case, my id would surely be trying to help me come round…so it made some sort of sense to follow the trail it was leaving for me; however tortuous. Didn't it? Maybe I read too much sci-fi.

I sucked a sweet. Two middle-aged Cockney women were chatting away behind me. I let myself drift into their conversation.

"When's it due?" said the smaller, rounder woman.

"'Oo knows?" her taller, skinny companion replied, her voice bending like her paper thin body in the fresh morning wind. "I waited 'ere two days once fer a bloody 75 bus."

"But the 75 don't come to this stop."

"I know, terrible service, innit?"

The stark logic of her statement had stunned the smaller woman into silence, but not for long. "It's this Coalition," she said. "They're using all the buses for transporting asylum seekers."

"Oh, I know."

"Y'know they say that if every 'sylum seeker in Britain joined hands they could circle the entire M25."

"That'd be 'ard to do though."

"What?"

"Getting them all to 'old 'ands an' circle the M25. I mean, that would be a very time-consumin' process. Say you started at the Dartford Crossing, you'd prob'ly only get as far the A2 before the first ones 'ad to stop 'oldin' 'ands and go for a Jimmy. Then there'd be tea breaks, dinner breaks…it'd be a nightmare to organize. An' what if one fell over? If they were standing too close together they might all go over, like dominoes."

"That's why they keep 'em in 'otels, I shouldn't wonder. They come straight orf the boat at Dover from Albania an' Bosnia an' Kathmandu, on the bus and straight on to the Ritz..."

A lengthy diatribe followed with the taller woman claiming that David Cameron had commandeered every other floor of London's plushest hotels for the exclusive use of asylum seekers, who over-indulge on room service and for cultural reasons crap in the baths. The other floors were used, she patiently explained, by adulterous footballers, celebrities, Page 3 girls, MPs, soap stars and fake Sheiks for "Shaggin' an' cocaine orgies. All they ever think about. Sex 'n' drugs. Shaggin' each other's brains out I shouldn't wonder and then racing to the phones to flog their sordid stories to the Sunday papers. Full of filth and bad language they are. You never get nuffin' normal in them papers. Filthy rags. Just footballers and bits of tarts out of soap operas shaggin' each other in all sorts of immoral places."

"What," the other woman ventured gingerly. "On ironing boards?"

"No. In places...places I wouldn't even let Bert touch let alone stick his old peculiar."

"Perverts," said the smaller woman wistfully.

"And the papers lap it up. They never talk about nuffin' that matters, like the Middle East or the energy crisis."

"My Sid's 'ad an energy crisis ever since we got married..."

"No-one has any time to debate anyfin' sensible. I turn the telly off and listen to that TalkSport, now that is an education an' no mistake. There was a fella on there 'oo had proof that the E numbers in curry are turning people into militants."

"Always 'ad a stomach ache or felt too tired."

"That's why all the tube drivers are always on strike, cos they have to make do with take-aways. And the ones at Aldgate are the most militant cos that's right on top of Brick Lane. Always full of rhetoric, they are."

"That's all 'e 'ad in 'is strides, rhetoric. 'E talked a good bunk-up; I'll give 'im that..."

"And they get paid a fortune. My Bert knows a tube driver on £1,500 a week and they don't get taxed."

"You know he ain't been 'ome since last weekend. He went to see some cowboy film with Dale, his friend from the fishing club, and ain't been back. I spect there's a queue."

"Fifteen hundred pound a week but they still keep moaning. It's strike strike strike. And they envy the rich so much. I can't understand it. The rich need all their money. They 'ave to change clothes several times a day and entertain important foreigners."

"My Sid never used to change his pants for weeks on end but since 'e met that Dale 'e seems to 'ave changed. 'E's gone from baggy old y-fronts to tight white Joe Snyder thongs. 'E's joined the Lib Dems. And 'e smells different...'ard to explain...perfumed, almost feminine...Still, he's a very clever man that Dale. He says 'e's discovered a new day of the week between Wednesday and Fursday, what's been hidden from us by the military-industrial complex since the dawn of time..."

I'd heard enough. "Excuse me ladies, can you tell me, is it normal to have to wait this long here for a bus?"

"Eh?" they said as one.

"I mean, I've been here over six hours and you must have been here for two or three. Is there some sort of industrial action today?"

"Bloody strikers," muttered the taller woman. "If it's not asylum seekers an' strikers, it's George Osborne stealin' the pasties from the mouths of our babies. Oily-looking, squeaky-voiced posh Eton bastard."

She lowered her voice. "He's actually a lizard y'know, Dale's got proof."

I looked at her properly for the first time. She looked like an anorexic Dot Cotton. Her face looked weatherproofed for disappointment. Her skin was amazingly tight, and it was stretched so thinly over her lean features it made the woman looked cadaverous.

"Where 'ave you got to get to, saucy?" asked the smaller woman, who had the red cheeks of a seaside postcard landlady and the trusting eyes of a baby seal.

"New Cross Road."

"Ah, the number 5," the tall woman remarked. "That's a bit far to walk," she continued.

"Oh, it's a lovely walk," enthused her friend. "I bet you love walking don'tcha, boy? You look a very 'ealthy young man." She leaned forward and stroked my hand. "Very physical." She winked.

"Er, I don't mind exercise," I said cautiously.

"I bet you don't."

"I used to love walking," the taller woman said. "I'd walk from Eltham, down to New Eltham, then on to Sidcup, Petts Wood and down to St Mary's Cray. Lovely. Then all the pykies moved in and spoilt the area. Ruined it they did, the big hairy brutes. And the men weren't much better. That was the only 'oliday we ever 'ad."

"My Sid never took me on 'oliday once. Not even on 'oneymoon. He said the working classes didn't deserve 'olidays 'cos we weren't cultured enough to enjoy them. He used to just go off and fish for weekends with 'is friends from the scout group. Were you ever a scout, boy?"

"No I'm afraid not."

"Oh. Shame. I could picture you as a sixer…standing there with yer lovely little woggle in yer hand."

She squeezed my left bicep and I shifted uneasily.

"Have you ever made love to an older woman, boy?"

"Pardon?

"'Ave you taken a mature lady roughly over her ironin' board?"

"Er, no. No I haven't."

She grabbed my hand again. "You don't know what you're missing," she said, her eye-lids fluttering like butterfly wings.

"P-p-probably not. Excuse me. I'm just going to have another look at the time table."

"Well if you've got the time, love, I've got the table."

She cackled so much she nearly choked.

"'Ere," said the taller woman. "'ave you heard this about that Red Tommy?"

"Oo?" her friend wheezed as she struggled to get her breath.

"That terrorist fella the police are looking for. Turns out he's working for Bin Laden's lot and look, he's part of a cell who was planning to blow up the Queen. Look..." She brandished a copy of *The Sun.*

"Hasn't 'e got nice eyes?" said her smaller friend.

"Dial Teen For Terror," the tall woman read. "Scrimbo, the teenage fugitive wanted for attempted murder..."

Shit. This was getting too close for comfort. I had to get out of this queue; maybe change my appearance. There was a newsagents a few doors down. If they sold scissors, and an A – Z, I could cut my hair and find my way on foot. I slipped away from the queue and strode briskly to the Newington News paper shop. My face was on every front page. Most newspapers had used a picture of me beaming angelically in my old school uniform with irritatingly chubby cheeks. 'Curfew demand to crack down on insurgents' thundered *The Daily Telegraph.* 'Iraqi Link To London Terror' asserted *The Times.* 'Cherry Bomb! Virgin Scrimbo Will Kill For Sex!' reported the *Daily Star.* Priceless. *The Mirror* had an analysis of my i-pod by Nick Hornby, which was surprising as I had never owned one.

"Can I help you?"

The clipped vowels managed to load even this innocuous phrase with disapproval. I turned to see the austere face of Ernest Flett, a grey man of indeterminate middle age, staring at me through thick spectacles.

"I was, erh, I was, ah, I was wondering if you sold scissors."

"No "

"Disposable razors?"

"No."

"Stanley knives?"

"Why would I?"

"Well a lot of corner shops...," I began.

"This is a newsagent's, not a corner shop nor a barber shop; neither is it a haberdasher's. I sell newspapers, magazines, confectionary, tobacco, cigarettes, soft drinks and Lottery tickets. If I can interest you in any of the aforementioned items then your presence is most welcome. If not, then I bid you good-day."

"Do you stock the A-Z?"

"Does this look like a bookshop? Is it a lending library? Can you see the word 'Bibliotheque' on display anywhere?"

"It's just that I've been waiting an awfully long time for a bus and I don't really know the Elephant."

"It's Newington."

"Pardon?"

"This area is Newington. Not the Elephant."

"I see. Thank you. But would you know, sir, if there is a mini cab office in walking distance?"

"There is not, for the simple reason that the roads in this area are premium congestion, which means they are not for use by private cars in any capacity. This is Authority policy to encourage the use of public transport."

"Ah yes, very good. Stamp out the car, save the planet and all that. Well I'm all for the Greens, but it doesn't make life too easy when there are no buses about."

Flett shot me a look more disapproving than the last. "Life is not supposed to be easy," he said pompously. "In fact the rarity of the buses is also Authority policy. It gives troubled commuters the gift of time, the most precious commodity in our modern world. Did you not realise that buses are irregular deliberately? It's incredibly well thought out. I mean, while you're waiting several hours for a bus what can you do but think? The wonder of nature, the human lot, what is infinity, is there a God? We're talking the big questions here. And when you get on the bus there are pamphlets full of answers. It's stealth education for the advancement of the masses. You should speak to my brother-in-law, Reginald. He wrote an Authority pamphlet on the matter: The Philosophy of London Transport."

"Is that true?"

Flett sighed. "Is anything actually true, or is truth just what it suits us to believe in? What seems true to our narrow human perception may just be a convenient myth sugar-coated with ignorance or indolence…"

As he jabbered on, I quietly slipped out to the street. The queue now stretched as far as my eyes could see. This would never do. I'd phone for a cab, and borrow the money to pay for it when I got to Jimmy-Jinnee's. Was he related to Louie Louie, I wondered? "Louie, Louie," I sang softly. "Oh no, me gotta go..."

There was a quaint old-fashioned red phone box a few yards up the road, which was odd, but in the context of everything else that had happened not odd enough to raise an eyebrow. Inside, I reached for the yellow pages but was immediately distracted by the usual array of prostitutes' calling cards: 'Young Thai girl! Exotic massage!' boasted one. 'Beautiful French butterfly, needs mounting', suggested another. 'Private care nurse, I will dribble my extra-virgin olive oil on your swelling.'

One bold black and white card caught my eye. It featured a fierce-looking brunette in stockings and a corset carrying a cane. It bore the legend: 'Madam O will beat naughty boys for six.' I stared at the image for a moment too long and felt myself being drawn into. "No," I moaned. "There isn't time..."

"Well you had better make time," said a stern female voice. I was inside the card and Madam O was striking her palm with her cane. "You are late for detention."

She was strikingly pretty, like a young Carla Bruni.

"I'm so sorry," I stuttered. "But I have an appointment. I'm supposed to be in New Cross, and I'm afraid I have no money."

"So no time for detention and no money to pay," she said sternly. "You really are a naughty boy, aren't you?"

"Yes, Ma'am, I suppose I..."

"Drop your trousers!"

"But, I..."

"No buts, boy, drop your trousers and bend over that desk. You've wasted my time and I demand payment."

Reluctantly I did as I was bid.

"What's this?" Madam O, put her hand down the back of my boxers and removed a school book that had appeared from nowhere. "You'll get an extra two strokes for that. Drop your pants too."

"I..."

"DO IT!"

I obeyed and the thrashing began. After six strokes my buttocks felt numb but the consequences were hard to avoid.

"We'll deal with that upstart next time," she said, in a voice full of promise.

"Yes Ma'am."

"So make sure you bring your pocket money like a good pupil. Now, New Cross, you say? You'd better get going. There are fifteen buses due immediately." And with that she placed a sharp stiletto on my posterior and pushed me back into the phone box.

True enough buses were pulling up at the stop. I fell out, yanking up my trousers and pants like a sitcom adulterer and pelted for it. The people in the queue were fighting for a place on the first three vehicles. A fourth was just arriving behind. By running parallel with the scrum-like head of the crowd I managed to jump on ahead of them just as the doors opened. A recorded message greeted us: "Marxists upstairs rear, existentialists and various upstairs front, Nietzscheans downstairs, followers of Wittgenstein take the lower rear seats, neo-Kantians please yourselves."

A philosophy bus!

"Why isn't there a set place for neo-Kantians?" asked an irate man in a grubby mac.

"Because of the unresolved dualism at the heart of neo-Kantian thought," replied the driver with a world-weary sigh.

"Excuse me, sir," I said. "Do you pass New Cross Road?"

"As often as possible, son. I'll give you a shout when we're there."

I went upstairs. The Marxists were an unruly looking bunch. A gang of Stalinists in the back seats were glaring menacingly at four Trots seated two rows in front of them, while a lone Maoist tormented a progressive vicar with a sharpened chop stick. Gingerly, for my behind still throbbed with pleasant pain, I sat next to a bald man in a shabby suit sitting about halfway down the bus. True enough there were well-thumbed pamphlets chained to the back of all the seats, but none of the other passengers were taking any notice of them. A tough-looking kid in a parka wearing an incongruent Morrissey t-shirt was tearing strips from the cover of his to make a spliff.

There were small signs over some of the other rows proclaiming 'Hegel', 'Blok', 'Gierke', 'Splenger', 'Sartre', 'Derrida' and so on; but only the Marxists and the Corporatists seemed to be in the correct seats. The 'postmodernists' were a couple of pensioners reading *The Sun.*

"Good isn't it?" the small bald man said to me.

"Pardon?"

"I said, it's all rather good isn't it, to see the public taking to the Authority's philosophy out-reach."

"Yes. Very."

"Healy is the name, Gerald Healy. I work for the Authority, in the Equality Department."

He proffered out a sweaty palm which I shook reluctantly.

"Tom, erh, Terence," I said. "Terence…" I looked around for inspiration. Foucault? No that wouldn't do. "Russell," I said finally. "As in Bertrand, although I feel a bit of a Kant at the moment."

"Delighted to meet you Mr. Russell. Would you care to see our next initiative?" He produced some hand-written pages of notes. "Now, let's see, I know this will interest you. Yes. We've made some major breakthroughs on the equality trail. It's a set fee to travel anywhere on a London bus, but that isn't really equal is it? For a system of true equality we need to achieve human parity. Are you with me?"

"Not really," I stuttered

"Well, how can people be equal when some are taller than others? It won't do at all. So from September this year we will implement an equal height rule. Anyone shorter than the recommended height will be given a choice of platform shoes and/or a few sessions on the municipal rack. Under Health and Safety supervision of course. How tall are you?"

"Six foot one."

"Well let's say the height we decide on is precisely six feet. You're an inch too tall. So we'd issue you with braces to give you a slight stoop. The taller you are, the tighter the braces. In extreme cases we'd also line citizens' jackets with fishing weights. Short people will get built-up shoes. Do you see? Similarly, we will introduce solutions to weight inequities. Those men fatter than thirteen stones will be given the option of dieting or liposuction. Anyone lighter will be fattened up or fitted with weights before they are permitted to travel. Equality is our goal and as you can see it is quite within our reach."

He sat back and smiled.

"What about other inequalities?" I asked. "Eye colour, nose size, skin pigmentation, gender? You can't legislate those out of existence."

"By golly you're right!" Healy exclaimed. "Even with size and weight fixed, bigots will find something else to target. Yes…" He started to scribble. "Given time and a progressive programme of interbreeding we can eliminate so-called ethnic differences. But if we apply a programme of cosmetic surgery and tanning to new-born babies we can speed up the process, at least superficially. I shall recommend it. We shall institute the Age of Beige! Only when humankind is perfectly identical can true equality be achieved."

"And mental equality?"

"Yes of course, we're already on course for that with comprehensive schooling." Healy leaned forward and touched his nose with a wink. "No-one too clever, no-one too dim. Just as it should be. I like the way you're thinking, Terence, you have the makings of a visionary. A very bright boy, but not too bright I hope." He laughed like a benign uncle. "I'd like you to come and work with me. Who do you work for now?"

"Um, the Authority."

"Really, I may know your superior. What is their name?"

"Oh, you probably won't."

"Come on, boy."

"Er, Clarkson, Brian Clarkson."

Healy began to write out the name. "B-r-i…wait a minute," he said. "Isn't that the fellow who was so viciously beaten by some neo-fascist thug of an employee recently? Some BNP sleeper agent, I believe. A most distressing case."

"Well, no, I heard there was a little trouble, but it was all a big misunderstanding..."

"A little trouble? Have you gone raving mad? There was an arson attack, a near insurrection. We were on the verge of absolute chaos." Healy produced a copy of the *Guardian* from his suit pocket. "Look at this," he jabbed at the story, reading 'Police removed literature from Scrimshaw's South London home. According to Searchlight this included The Anarchist Cookbook and hate leaflets produced by an American neo-Nazi sect called The National Alliance'..."

"But that's impossible."

"Why do you say that? Hold on a minute." Healy held the newspaper alongside my face. "It's you!" he said, adding with a shout: "The anarchist insurgent. Here, here on this bus!"

Healy began to strike me with his newspaper. "Fascist!" he screamed. "Anarchist!"

"Well, he can hardly be both," said an indignant Trotskyist with a plumy voice as I rolled on the floor.

"This man is a revolutionary," shouted Healy.

"Solidarity, brother!" Plumy replied, punching Healy on the nose.

"Isn't that the arsonist?" snorted a Stalinist.

"This man is being persecuted by the Cameron/Obama criminal war alliance," declared another Trot, a raven-haired female with an equally cut-glass accent and a magnificent cleavage.

"He's an infantile ultra-Leftist!" screamed the Maoist.

"And you, comrade, are a falsifier of Lenin," my protector exclaimed.

"Spartist!"

Within seconds the air was filled with insults as the Marxists began to fight each other. I began to crawl away from the fracas, noticing that the beautiful red-haired revolutionary was now passionately kissing a suave-looking Stalinist.

"Look at them," said a man in the seat in front. "They hate one another but they can't fight the love. He's the thesis, she's the antithesis and this is the synthesis. It's Hegelianism in action, pure and perfect. It's beautiful!"

Standing by the top of the stairs, I watched him reach for his handkerchief and dab at his eyes.

"Next stop for New Cross Road," shouted the bus driver." At which point, the lout in the parka got to his feet and helpfully kicked me down the stairs. The bus pulled up at a stop.

"New Cross, gateway to the sarf!" the driver hollered. I rolled out through the doors and breathed a premature sigh of relief. But no, Healy had the window open and was shouting "It's the terrorist!" at the top of his voice. Two motorcycle cops sipping cappuccinos outside an Italian café looked over and started to walk towards me. One of them had a layer of froth on his upper lip giving the impression of having a creamy moustache. Either that or the two were much closer than they looked.

I turned and ran. The cops ran too. Within moments a mob had formed behind me chanting "Kill! Kill! Kill!" They had just begun to sing "Burn, burn, burn the bastard!" when I turned into a bustling street market. The sheer numbers of shoppers slowed down my pursuers whose voices were swallowed up by the noise. I ran down side-streets, through shops, and over stalls until I tripped turning a corner and smashed my forehead on the corner of an old record stall called Vinyl Resting Place.

For a moment I saw stars, but as my head cleared I realised there was a figure in a superhero costume beaming down at me.

"Superman?" I said softly.

"No, no. Harold Starks, late of Fathers 4 Justice, now of the splinter group Fathers 4 Gotten. Are you OK, boy?"

His breath spelt pleasantly of whisky and beer.

"I'm in trouble, I'm innocent, but the police…"

"Say no more, brother," said Harold with a sigh. "You're a male so naturally the system seeks to persecute you. How can I help?"

I struggled to his feet and looked up the road. The two cops and their lynch mob were about thirty feet away and closing. I gripped Harold by the arm and said: "Something very strange is about to happen." I picked up an album at random from the stall.

"In a moment, you won't see me, but I need you to take this album and walk out of this market. When you're clear of here and there is no-one about, I want you to start coughing. Will you do that for me?"

"Well, yes…"

"Good, no time to explain. Catch this album when it drops."

I stared at the cover. It was Never Mind by Nirvana. Trust me to pick a wet one. I concentrated on the image of the baby in the pool and vanished into it. Harold, though shocked, caught the LP and started walking.

"Oi," shouted the Turkish stall-holder. "Stop thief!"

Harold scarpered. A whole new mob of stall-holders began to chase him. After a hundred yards or so, he coughed loudly, chucked the Nirvana album into an alley and escaped by climbing a fire escape. The angry stall-holder found his LP next to a dozy looking youngster in soaking wet clothes pointing skywards as a caped figure leapt from one building to the next. Then some noisy men appeared with their cameras flashing.

It was the last thing I saw before I passed out.

***

I was back in the original dream, but something had changed. This time it didn't stop. I went through all the usual aspects of it, up to and including the ill-fated kiss with the dissolving Freeje clone – surely symbolizing some deep-rooted psychological fear of the female, I'd decided based entirely on my memories of Frasier scripts.

The body of my would-be lover now lay bubbling at my feet. It looked like simmering placenta and smelt like rotting fish-heads. I heard the wolf louder than before, it seemed to be getting closer. My flesh still crawled from her sticky embrace, but at least the burning sensation had ended. Rubbing my tingling arms, I surveyed the barren landscape noticing again the distant New Cross platform sign. In the sunset, the sky was losing its washed denim look and taking on a deep purple glow. Any other time, the view would have been breathtaking. Now it filled me with foreboding.

Suddenly the pool at my feet reached boiling point. The features of Eddie, Iron Maiden's monstrous mascot, were forming beneath the surface. Within seconds, the head had become three-dimensional, bursting out of its liquid womb and spouting a body that swelled up to twice my size. The monster's eyes were dark holes, wells of hate. Eddie's hands closed around my neck and squeezed. As I began to lose consciousness, I heard singing: *'Wine is fine, but whisky's quicker...'*

Ozzy? Or the Oz-Troll? Eddie released his grip. I could hear the rock god, and then I saw him. It wasn't the troll. This Ozzy was bigger than Eddie, taller, stronger. He came roaring out of the distance, grinning like a madman and barking at the rising moon. He was sky-high. Ozzy raised his right foot and brought it crashing down on Eddie. The monster's body squashed out like Play-dough before slowly shrinking back into shape. Dazed, Eddie lurched off, yelping.

"Thanks Oz," I gasped. Ozzy's fist closed around my ankles. I was acutely aware of the dampness of my legs and the howling of the wolf. I looked to my right and for the first time, I saw the beast in all its ferocious glory.

"Ozzy, look," I said.

"This is too soon," Ozzy slurred. "You have things to see first, things to learn…"

In the background, Randy Rhodes's guitar exploded in a never-ending solo as the gigantic Ozzy Osbourne hauled my body into the air, spinning me round like an Olympic hammer, before launching me up and into space….

I woke up with a start.

***

Keziah had asked Mark and Matty to meet her in the Gambadella's, then changed her mind and made it the British Oak down the bottom end of Shooter's Hill instead. No-one knew them in the Oak. Going in Gambadella's after the trial would be to invite a Spanish Inquisition from the regulars and endure yet more tedious speculation about Tom's whereabouts and motivation. The friends assembled straight from work, sat in a corner and spoke in whispers.

"Do you think he's OK?" asked Keziah for the seventy-second time anxiously between sips of diet cola.

"He'll be fine," Mark assured her, nursing a half.

"Yeah," said Matty. "Fine. I hope."

"Where do you think he is?"

"No idea."

"I'm worried. Could he be with friends?"

"We're his friends, dummy."

"Maybe he's tucked up with what's-her-face from the gig," Matt laughed. "Old Freeje feel-me touch-me heal-me."

"Matt, this is serious," said Keziah. "We've got to help him."

"How?"

"He could be anywhere," Mark said sadly.

"The police will be after him," said Matt.

"And so should we be."

"But we don't know where to look."

"Nor will anyone else."

"She's right mate, we should do something."

"How much money have you got?" Keziah asked.

"About twenty quid till pay day," replied Mark. "Matt?"

"A pony."

"I've got a few hundred saved at home. Here's what we do. Pool the money, tell our parents we're going off on a camping weekend or something, and start looking. Can you borrow a car, Mark?"

"Probably but I haven't passed my test."

"That's the least of our worries."

"We'll start on Friday night. Sleep in the car if we have to. And leave our mobiles on at all times, OK?"

"You're the boss."

"I like her when she's strict."

"Be quiet or I'll slap your legs."

"Yes miss."

"Friday night, then?"

"Straight after work."

"Deal."

"You really got a few hundred quid tucked away, Kez?" asked Matt.

"Yeah, I always save a fiver a week."

"Well get a round in, babe."

"Pig."

Matt laughed. "The price of bacon, that's no insult."

***

"Are you OK?" A hand was shaking me. "You're soaking wet?" A West Indian man with a friendly face was talking. "Are you all right?"

"I'm fine," I replied.

"I know who you are," the man whispered. "I've seen you in the papers."

Shit. "None of it is true," I stuttered.

"It's OK, I believe you. I know the papers tell lies. My name is Lynval, but everyone calls me Len. I will help you. Do you need a doctor? My GP is a good man. He is Dr Wabba W. Wabba."

"What does the W stand for?" I asked, still slightly dazed.

"Wabba. Or there's Dr. Alimantado, his surgery is nearer, actually."

"No, no, I'm not hurt, thanks Len. I need to get somewhere."

"I have clothes for you. Dry clothes, from my sister's stall. Look…"

He handed me a burqa. "I am not taking the Mick. The police are looking for a young white male, with this, and this" – he produced a veil – "you will pass for a female." Len smiled. "I could have got you a nice, red sari, but you would probably have attracted too much attention."

"Yes…," I said uncertainly, deciding wisely against adding the sari with a fringe on top gag.

"Where must you get to?"

"New Cross Road."

"It's not far, but there is somewhere you must go first. Are you a Christian, Thomas?"

"I suppose."

"If you don't have medical assistance, you must have spiritual guidance. You are in great danger. You must not face it alone."

"I have friends..."

"Yes, yes, all in good time. Nothing is too important to stand between a man and his God. But first you need food and you need rest. You still have an awfully long way to go...in every sense. Come now, get dressed. We must hurry."

Len walked a few hundred yards to a council flat, with me traipsing a respectful few feet behind in my burqa. At the sparsely furnished flat, he and his quiet wife Sunita - "call me Sue" – cooked me curried goat, and then let me shower and sleep. At nightfall, Len took me back out in my own clothes which Sue had washed and ironed, and drove me in his old Vauxhall Cresta to a Church, with even older Ska songs playing on the battered old cassette player: Laurel Aitken, Earnest Ranglin, Max Romeo, Eric 'Monty' Morris.

At the traffic lights, I saw enough of the *Evening Standard* front page to laugh, and to curse. The main picture was of Superman leaping from building to building with the headline: 'Super Yob', sub-head: 'Militant fathers' spark London riot...Ex-wife says 'superhero' "flies like a bird, drinks like a fish".'

Less funny was the banner screaming: 'Transvestite Tom's links to Islamic State – inside.' Where had they got that shot of me? 'Burqa Berk! Gok Wan on why the Tommy look is passé.' Gok Wan! Not for nothing was his name an anagram of Go Wank.

The lights changed. Len turned the corner and pulled up outside a sign that said 'St Mary's, Church of the C.G.' What was that, some kind of Catholic thing? I didn't have the heart to tell him he was C of E.

"Your journey will be long, and you can be certain that much darkness is still ahead," Len said grimly. "It would be helpful to have a guiding light. Please, Thomas, I beg you try, for your sake, enter this Church, make your peace with God."

He smiled. I nodded and reluctantly went in. The first thing that hit me was the noise of the place; the church was packed, and when I looked more closely I noticed the entire congregation were knocking back alcohol. There was a well-stocked bar that ran along the entire right-hand side of the church, with well-stacked barmaids behind it serving the thirsty. Almost immediately a man clambered up onto it and began to blast the barmaids' tight tops with water. The crowd roared their approval.

"Hallelujah!" shouted the man.

"Praise the Lord!" replied the congregation.

The guy with the gun was wearing a diamond-studded dog collar.

"This is the new Mark 3 Holy Water Super-Squirt Soaker, yours for just £19.99 at the Church store," he announced over a microphone. "Be sure to buy one while stocks last, go on, give the missus a treat, you know you will."

The drunken flock cheered, and the priest soaked up their acclaim. He was charismatic and handsome, with perfect teeth – one of them pure gold - and a genial Southern Irish lilt to his accent. He jumped back down behind the bar and rang the bell.

"That's it folks, time to go, drink up."

The congregation booed.

"Now come on, you can still get the Last Supper in the church hall, it's the loaves and fishes special tonight, and be sure to come back on Sunday for the new miracle."

"I hope it's better than the last one," murmured a man to my left.

"What wash it?" slurred an inebriated woman. "I'm new here."

"He sawed the verger in half."

"It was worse last Easter," grumbled another man. "He promised us three miracles for the price of two, but they were only card-tricks and the grand finale, 'Finding the Virgin Mary' turned out to be a game of Chase The Lady'."

I hid in the pews to the front left of the church and waited for it to empty out. Killing time, I flicked through a bible and was shocked to find it had a colour centre-fold, 'Miss Deuteronomy,

2011'. 'Thy rod and staff they comfort me, big boy' was the caption.

On other pages I found adverts for exclusive COCG films on DVD including The Born-Again Supremacy, Live & Let Diocese, Holy Ghost-Busters and the groan-inducing How To Train Your Deacon.

It even offered massages. There was the 'Superior Massage', apparently performed by 'Cork's fiercest' Mother Superior Flora 'The Flagellator' O'Flaherty with the tag-line 'Nun but the brave', and Junior Massages for under-15s performed free of charge by the unsavoury sounding visiting Irish priest Peadar O'Fuile from Galway's Willyrogue Island. What the...?

Slowly the church cleared. First the drinkers, then the barmaids, until there was only one scruffy wreck of the man sitting alone at the back. The priest approached him. "Come on now, finish that prayer please sir. I can't abide drunks on the premises after hours. Hurry along or I'll be fining yer four Hail Marys and three Pete Dohertys."

"Father O'Golding?" he replied.

"Yes my son..."

"I've come for help."

"Go on."

"I've fallen on hard times, could you spare a few bob from the church collecting plate for a poor sinner seeking to repent?"

"Go on, get off with you," O'Golding snapped. "You miserable wretch, what do you think I'm running here, some kind of charity?"

"I knew it," snapped the man, who leapt to his feet, and ripped off his top to reveal a dog collar of his own. "Edward Campillo, Church Police," he snarled. "We knew you had a racket going on here O'Golding, but we weren't sure how bent you were until now."

The priest smiled. "Bent?" he said. "I'm not sure what you mean, Father Campillo. It may be that you've seen me raising some cash here tonight but it all goes to the Church."

"You've send nothing through to us for over a year, not one single donation."

"Ah yes," he said. "But we have needs here to attend to first. There's a terrible hole in the church roof that requires urgent attention."

His grin grew wryer; his eyes were on full sparkle.

"I don't believe you."

"Come, I'll show you."

O'Golding led the inquisitive Campillo through a door to the left of the altar. I followed – at a distance. They climbed the stairs to the roof. Neither I nor Mr 'God Plod' noticed the priest pull a cord that triggered a mechanism causing the church roof to part like the Red Sea.

"It's a terrible mess," said O'Golding. "It is going to take thousands more to put right."

"How did it happen?" asked Campillo.

"I believe it was t'ieves stripping the roof of lead; one of them must have fallen through, but it's caused great structural damage. Come step on to this beam and take a closer look."

As Campillo climbed up, O'Golding casually pushed him to his death. Startled, I stepped backwards, missed my footing and fell with a thud.

"Who's there?" asked the priest.

"Erh, my name's Thomas, I'm sorry, I was just looking for guidance."

"Did you see what just occurred?"

"Nnno."

"A terrible tragedy. A man has just taken his own life. What an awful waste."

"That's shocking, father…?"

The priest held out his hand. "Patrick Thaddeus O'Golding, how can I help?"

"Will you take my confession, father."

"We run a 'don't-ask, don't-confess' policy here, my son. '"Do what thou wilt shall be the whole of the Law'."

"Wasn't that Alistair Crowley?"

"Yes."

"A Satanist?"

"What was Lucifer but a fallen angel? We need to be less judgemental, more inclusive."

We walked back down the stairs.

"I've never seen a church like this," I said nervously. "What does it stand for 'Church of C.G.' Catholic God?"

"No Corporate Gratification," O'Golding smiled. "My church is geared to the needs of the 21st Century. Never mind the meek, I say blessed are the strong, blessed are the money-makers. Our holy spirit is the zeitgeist, Tommy boy, and our God is global capitalism. By recognising the true nature of man, I am placing religion back where it belongs – not sulking at the back disapproving of everything like most modern clergy, but leading from the front in the proud name of profit and progress."

"Amen to that." I said hoping the sarcasm was lost on him.

"Amen, indeed. And our approval is not enough; I believe the Church must be part of the invigorating process that is unfettered commercialism. We must be seen to make money too, as a spiritual beacon for the faithful. God isn't dead, Thomas, he's just been privatised."

"Isn't there a line in the Bible about rich men, camels and needles?"

"Heard it! That's so first century, man."

"But Jesus said…"

"Jesus shmeezus, the man only had twelve disciples! I've got hundreds and I want millions! You have to stop living in the past, Tom, and embrace the faith. Look…"

O'Golding led me into his office. There was an open fire roaring in the grate, and a shelf full of religious icons.

"Sit," said the priest as he started rooting around in his desk. "Now, what you've seen tonight is just the start. Look at my plans for the future."

The priest produced a glossy catalogue. "Here are some of my new products. Inflatable nuns! Vibrating mitres! We're moving into the Sex market. Look, here's my new magazine, Repenthouse, with gorgeous pouting choir girls – and boys, we don't discriminate!"

I flicked through it stopping at a revealing picture of 'Bernadette, 15' was captioned 'In your right hand there are pleasures for ever – Psalm 16:11'. Over the page, the priest posed with 'Sandra, 18' under the headline 'Open wide your mouth and I will fill it – Psalm 81:10'.

He snatched it back. "No free reads, we're not a lending library. But if you buy a copy you'll find photos of our topless prayer meetings on the centre spread. We're building our own off-licence. You'll like this, it's called Judas's Carry-Out! Do you see? Judas's Carry-out!"

Even as a lover of poor puns this made me wince.

"We're setting up a website God.com too," he continued. "A faith-based emporium for all your spiritual knickknacks."

"How did it come to this?" I asked, aghast.

"Well I started by selling commercial breaks in the Sunday sermon, that went down well, so I sublet the less useful parts of the Church to InterFlora, Relate and Co-op Funerals – just offering a useful after-sales service, y'see. Then I had a range of hand-crafted wooden furniture 'just as the holy carpenter would have made'. We've got Christian traffic wardens and Happy Clampers. Now we're moving in to curses too."

He gave me a leaflet which read 'See your ex burn in hell, £1,000 will guarantee eternal damnation to your enemies. PLUS! £10,000 to book your place in Heaven NOW! Reasonable HP terms available on request.' On the back of it was an advert for Theo Jinnee, Private Investigator etc etc

"Impressed?"

I thought hard about what to say next. The priest, who had scooped to pick up a small grey mouse from the floor, was smiling.

"I'm thinking of having a slogan: 'The church that pays a divine dividend'. It's good, is it not?"

"I really don't think it's good or impressive in any way," I said finally. "This is just cheating people."

"Ho, an unbeliever!"

"I certainly don't believe greed is good."

"Greed is God!" spat the priest as he swung the mouse by its tail. "You atheists make me sick. You're all just searching in the dark for nothing."

"Looks like you've been searching in the dark for nothing too, Father," I said. "But you've found it."

O'Golding glared. "I know you," he said slowly. "You're that rebel chap who's been in all the papers."

"Yes…"

"What's to stop me ringing the police now and turning you in? I understand there's quite a tidy price on your head."

I didn't flinch. "I saw what you did earlier," I said.

"What?"

"I saw you push that poor man off the roof."

O'Golding smiled. "Oh yes I saw you do that too."

"What?"

"Who do you think the police will believe? A respected priest or a known malefactor?"

I stood up. "You filthy bastard," I said.

"Filthy rich bastard," replied the priest, slinging the mouse into the fire.

I turned and ran. The priest followed laughing as he dialled 999 on his iPhone. Neither of us noticed the mouse emerge from the fire with its tail ablaze. It ran over O'Golding's paperwork, starting a blaze that would raise the Church of Corporate Gratification to its ungodly foundations.

I burst out into the night air, breathless and panting. Len was waiting I jumped into the passenger seat and begged him to drive.

"How was your church?"

"A disaster."

"Not for you?"

"Not for me. Please drive."

Len started the car. "But you believe, don't you?"

"Sometimes. I dunno. I'm agnostic I suppose. Please can we get going…"

Len pulled away, with Fire Corner by Clancy Eccles playing softly and appropriately as we went. In the rear view mirror, I spotted O'Golding giving me the finger. And old biblical quotation, half remembered from Sunday school, popped into my head unbidden, something about 'your hands defiled with blood and your fingers with iniquity, your lips have spoken lies and your tongue hath muttered perversion...'

"Can we get to New Cross Road please?"

"Oh yes, man, that's where I'm heading."

"Thank you. But what about you, Len?" I asked. "Are you a Muslim?"

"I converted to Islam many years ago. But I hate the evil that is done in the name of the Prophet today. I have faith, but not one faith."

"Faith in what, though?"

Len paused. "Humanity," he said slowly.

"What, in this wicked, vindictive world? This vale of tears, with all the grasping and back-stabbing, the selfishness and hatred we see all around us?"

"All the time there are boys like you, with kind hearts and brave souls, there is reason to believe." Len smiled and accelerated.

Eight minutes later he turned into New Cross Road.

"Pull over there please my friend," I said. "I'll find it from here."

I got out of the car, and reached back to shake Len's hand.

"This thing we call life, it's big, and it's sprawling and it's messy," he said. "It is more than we can see and often more than we can know. Life can't be tidied up into neat compartments. It's a great adventure that spills over our plans and smudges our expectations. Most human beings will only ever experience life in three basic dimensions. Your gift, Thomas, although you're not yet aware of it, is to appreciate much more. To put it in terms you'll understand, you are experiencing life in broadband. Consider yourself blessed. And here, have a sweet."

The last three words reverberated with a cheery familiarity. I looked up. Len's smile made him look for a second uncannily like Jinnee. I started to speak but Len just winked, started up his Vauxhall and drove off.

The sun was rising over New Cross Road. It was a new dawn all right. I swallowed hard and began to walk slowly. All I had to do now was find the offices of Mr Theo Jinnee, PI. It was then I noticed that the road to my left was Lupino Lane...where *She* lived. Freeje. What to do? Not for the first time in my life when faced with a difficult decision, I passed the buck and let fate decide. The choice was starker than I could possibly know because as I would find out later it was quite literally one between heaven and hell. I tossed one of the few coins left in my pocket, tails for Mr Jinnee, heads for the lovely Freeje. The coin, by chance was one of the ones I'd scooped off the floor of the court. It had belonged to Judge Crook and it had two heads

Welcome To The House Of Fun

Day 14. My joy at finding Freeje's street began to crumble like a small child's sand castle in a hailstorm as soon as I started to walk down it. There were hard and hostile looking gangs on both sides of the road and most of the houses had boarded up windows which were blitzed with cluster bombs of graffiti. There were half-starved feral cats, scruffy snarling dogs, and at a distance, under a lamppost, loitered a small group of under-dressed over-perfumed women whose demeanour suggested that their affections were negotiable. They were moving slowly and sensuously to an obscure grime track. Had they been up all night?

I counted ahead and noticed that number 22 had a strange golden glow to it. It looked welcoming, it looked inviting, it looked like...good god, there was a bloke over there shooting up heroin in a front garden!

I stared a bit longer than I intended to, and not only because the garden gnome to his left was shaking his face in disgust. In the living room of the house another young fellow had hung himself; his visage was twisted into a portrait of ugliness and pain.

"Wha' you lookin' at bruv?" a black youth in blue sportswear approached me. He had a Russian army hat and white Nike Air Force 1 trainers. I also spotted the glint of a gold tooth.

"I, er, I'm just, ah…"

He was about my age but looked harder than Chinese algebra. The D.I.Y. crucifix tattoo between his eyes screamed young offenders' institute.

Just on cue, I heard Novelist speak the menacing words *'Man thinks he's brave, bold, blacked out on the baitest road, couple of YGs wanna take his phone…'*

"Why you think you can walk down my street for?" His accent was a strange mix of South London Cockney, Caribbean and Asian. Jafaican I think they call it. "Where's man gwoin'?"

I pointed ahead. "22," I said softly, deciding against attempting the accent. He had eyebrows like over-fed caterpillars.

"Then pay the toll, bruv," he replied, almost smiling. The rest of his gang had formed a circle around me, like buzzards waiting to tear the flesh off my happiness.

Where were my mates when I needed them? My 'homies'? I didn't have any cash or jewellery or even a phone to barter with. I was done for.

Across the road a different firm, largely Millwall hooligans in Stone Island windbreakers with a couple of old-fashioned skinheads in tow, began to laugh at my plight.

My tormentor was taller than me, with eyes like slits. He leaned in menacingly so I could smell his aftershave, which wasn't cheap. Here we go, I thought. Any minute now, the fists and the boots and then if I'm really unlucky the knives…

"Oi! 'E's with me," one of the prostitutes pushed through, and put her arm firmly around my shoulders. The mob parted for us like the Red Sea parting for Moses. We seemed to glide out of harm's way. "Thank you," I said. She kissed me softly on the cheek. I noticed her face for the first time. She looked oddly familiar. But before I could say any more she had pushed me down the front path. Number 22. I was here. At last.

I hope this was going to be worth it.

***

Inspector Arnott was not happy. He had been on this fifth Pina Colada, taking in the turquoise waters of St Lucia when the Met Commissioner had called to summon him back from paradise and put him in charge of the Scrimshaw case. "This is the biggest story in years, Arnie," he'd told him. "Catch this toe-rag and you'll be a national hero." The rest of the sentence was unspoken: don't catch him and you'll be a laughing stock, old son.

Arnott and his favourite sergeant, Arthur Lobon had reviewed the evidence at length. "It ain't good," Lobon had noted. The words fell from his tight, thin bloodless lips in a voice like rain falling on a discarded carpet. Thomas Scrimshaw was an enigma. He seemed to have the uncanny ability to vanish off the face of the earth whenever it suited him, re-appearing to commit some new atrocity at will. It was almost magical. "The little fucker even torched a church!"

Arnott shook his head. The investigating officers had nothing on Scrimshaw and it was just a matter of days before the press turned on them. He knew that there was only one way to prevent that – to establish an alternative narrative that TV news and newspaper editors would buy into. It didn't matter how phony it was as long as it made headlines. He had just the thing and he spelt it out at a well-attended press conference outside New Scotland Yard later that morning. Clearly Scrimshaw couldn't be doing this alone; he had to have a network of allies, sheltering him and keeping him supplied.

He'd had his intelligence experts study Scrimshaw's Facebook page and identify his closest friends. Not too surprisingly CCTV evidence revealed that three of them had attended the trial.

Arnott's authoritative performance at the press conference kept the rolling news channels busy all day. He'd widened the net, appealing to the public to turn in Thomas Scrimshaw's known confederates – Matt Cluer, Mark Gladbury and Kezia Smith. "The Big Three". It played well with the press pack and even earned him a selfie with a clearly impressed teenage girl. If in doubt, bluff.

***

Matt nearly choked on his pint when he saw his own face beaming out on Sky News. "The Big Three? It's lame, mate," he complained to Mark over the phone from the gent's. "Couldn't we be something sexier like The Teen Troika Of Terror? And did you see the way that Old Bill stoops? It's like his spine is a question mark asking the world: 'How the fuck did a twat like me get to be an inspector?'..."

"Buggery and backhanders probably," Mark said sourly. "Lunches and largess, with a side order of freemasonry." He thought for a moment and then carried on decisively. "Right, this is what we do. I'll get me uncle's jam-jar...you ring Kez, tell her she needs to withdraw all the cash she can ASAP and let's meet somewhere safe in about two hours' time."

"I know just the place. Right I'm on it like a car bonnet."

***

The front door was opened by a burly gent in bow tie and a tuxedo. He had the bearing of Carson from Downton Abbey.

"Thomas," he said. "We've been expecting you." The hall light framed his head, creating the illusion of a halo.

"Is this Freeje's house?" I asked a little lamely.

"It is indeed, but she is indisposed. Please come in."

As I stepped over the threshold I was overcome with a feeling of peace and safety so intense I almost glowed. The house seemed as safe and serene as a Surrey golf course in springtime.

"Are you her butler?"

"The likes of us don't have butlers," he smiled. "I'm Pete, I'm her mate."

"So why the fancy clobber?"

"I was just on my way to ballroom dancing in the conservatory, but that'll wait. Let me show you around."

The voice was London; Old London. It was the kind of accent you only heard in films like Passport To Pimlico. His breath smelt of malt whisky and Werther's Originals.

"Here's the notice-board," he said. "It'll give you some idea of the things we do." The notice-board was one of those fancy glass-fronted ones you see outside churches. Pinned up inside it was a mess of white postcards referring to poetry meetings, film classes, writers' workshops, a chess club, a basement comedy room, a science lab and a series of lectures being given by a Sue Sin on everything from economics to the history of the Music Hall.

"Sue Sin?" I said out loud.

"Short for syndicalist," said Peter, wrapping a big bear-like arm around my shoulder and steering up the stairs, past a poster promising a night of punk and Ska in the garden shed.

I must have been tired or distracted but there didn't seem to be any end to the house. We kept going up and up via different landings, past corridors that seemed to go on further than the eye could see. One level that we didn't stop at was designated as The Planetarium.

"How is this even possible?" I whispered.

"There's more to the working classes than meets the eye," Peter said simply.

We turned down a landing on our left. "Never open these doors on your own," he warned. "Now this is Freeje's room." He nodded towards a door that was slightly ajar. "She's just getting changed."

I glanced in as we passed the door and saw what looked like a large cocoon of fabric hanging from the ceiling.

"She'll take some time. You know what women are like." He gave a chuckle so deep and hearty that it seemed to make the landing shake. "Up here, lad."

The stairs were getting smaller and narrower, as if we were climbing up the inside of a helter-skelter. I was looking around for a mat to ride back down again. "This place is like the Tardis," I muttered.

"My father's house has many mansions," Peter said. "But we've only got the loft to go. Come on," he added cheerfully. "Come and meet Neighbourhood Watch." And then he laughed even louder.

Inside were three women who were studying CCTV footage of the surrounding buildings. "This is Deb, Jude and Jae," he said. "They're the day shift."

The women looked at me, smiled, and returned to their duties.

"They keep an eye out for criminal elements, and other more serious threats." He pointed out of a window. "Over there is Micklespill Lane, they get a lot of murders there…"

"Love thy neighbour always comes second to fear of your neighbour," I said mournfully.

"So Nietzsche said. We're more inclined towards the Ten Commandments here. But you can never be too careful." He pointed in the other direction. "Down that way is Itchycoo Park, full of drug dealers and drop-outs."

"Itchycoo Park? As in the Small Faces song?"

"They were with us. Arden, the manager, was on the other side."

More riddles. Pete seemed friendly enough but he was starting to get on my tits. One of the women was staring intently at a peculiar multi-screen device. "What's that?" I asked.

"The I.D.S."

Unlikely to stand for Iain Duncan Smith, I thought, hazarding the guess "Intrusion Detection System?"

"Inter-Dimensional Surfer. Known to the Egyptians as the Eye of Horus."

What? Horace who?

Peter noticed my confusion. "This is the beating heart of the multiverse," he said softly. "From here we can see every earth in every universe at any time since the Creation…"

"Do you mean the Big Bang?"

"Technically it was more like a Big Hand Job."

"Every earth? I don't understand."

"Well, thanks to the wonders of celestial space-time there are an infinite number of possible futures which of course are constantly changing. Every world is different, sometimes by fractions, other times by leagues. Why on one earth, two years hence, Britain will vote to leave the European Union! Could you imagine that happening here? Chairman Mandelson would never allow it."

This was doing my head in. I turned away. "When can I see Freeje?"

"All in good time, my son," Peter smiled. "Whoever is patient has great understanding."

***

For their own amusement, the "Big Three" rendezvoused in the café at the Museum of London, currently housing an exhibition based on Scotland Yard's Black Museum of crime.

"One day we could be in here," noted Mark. "Next to Crippen and the Krays."

"We could have just turned ourselves in, we've done nothing wrong!" Kez moaned quietly.

"Yeah but neither has Tom and look at the shit he's in." "Besides, where's the fun in that?" added Matt. Kez frowned. "I thought about him before I went to sleep last night and all I dreamt of were two ducks."

"Like he'd reach out to you in a dream!"

"All this started in his dreams, remember? It makes sense. What did you dream about?"

"Lambeth," replied Matt.

"Uh, the old time Music Hall," said Mark sheepishly.

"Random!"

"We do need to be out there looking for him."

"I see you've come prepared, Kez," said Matt. "Is that your get-away bag? What's in it, moody passports? Wads of foreign dosh?"

Keziah flipped open her duffle-bag. "Water, travel toiletries, toothbrushes, toothpaste, a torch, a compass, chewing gum, deodorant, a Swiss army knife, all the cash I could grab, some baked beans and spoons – just to tide us over."

"Very organised."

"She's a regular Dora the Explorer."

"We need to change our appearances too," said Kez. "So I've also brought hair dye and scissors."

"And lose our phones," Matt noted.

"Let's leave 'em on the Circle Line," laughed Mark. "That'll confuse the Keystone Cops."

"Some tow-rags will half-inch 'em and the Old Bill will be hunting for the wrong people," laughed Matt. He paused and thought. "We'll need to hole up somewhere safe for a while though."

"What like a squat?" Kez pulled a face.

"My uncles know people. They'll get us tucked up in some sweet little safe house in Deptford or Bermondsey, no questions asked."

"And then we can get on with finding Thomas."

"By the way, I messaged the Standard letters page from a moody email address referring to us as the Teen Troika of Terror," said Mark. "It was Matt's idea. Let's hope it catches on."

Keziah started to giggle. "Um, have you seen the front page today?"

Day 15. Inspector Arnott had been extremely pleased to make the splash of yesterday's London Evening Standard. "'Action This Day," says Iron Man Arnott' it had read, with an inset picture of him looking mean and moody next to an adoring teenage girl. He seemed forceful and in control; very much a man on a mission. But Arnott wasn't so pleased the following morning when The Mirror reproduced the same picture pointing out that the Inspector's selfie fan was actually Keziah Smith, the very subversive he was supposed to be hunting down. He was 'Anus of the Yard', according to a scathing opinion piece by Brian Reade, a jibe that stung more than the columnist could ever know...

Arnott's birth name had been Hugh Janus. He'd changed it by deed poll as soon as he was able in order to bury the misery of years of teenage teasing.

***

'Stop The Teen Troka of Terror', screamed that day's Standard; the front page headline for an imaginative piece on "the Scrimbo Gang" which described them as "teenage malcontents, Marxists and mischief makers" and comparing them to 1970s anarchists the Angry Brigade. The paper's thunderous editorial gave its backing to Inspector Arnott and concluded: *'Londoners will not tolerate Thomas Scrimshaw's flagrant violation of both the law and common decency. This evil teen is the Met's Most Wanted. It falls to all of us to be vigilant and keep on the watch for Scrimbo and his black-hearted mob. It is imperative that he is back behind bars as soon as possible.'*

***

Unaware of all this fuss, I had spent the day inside Freeje's house without actually meeting her. "Tomorrow," Peter assured me. "All will come good by tomorrow. Unless things go bad…" He led me to a room that was the size and shape of my own bedroom at home. "This is yours for as long as you want it," he said. "Sweet dreams." He closed the door but returned five minutes later with a steaming brew on a silver tray, holding it exactly like a man impersonating a butler might do, although of course he wasn't one. "Freeje asked me to give you this special nightcap," he said. "You'll like it."

I sipped it gingerly and my tongue exploding in competing flavours. It tasted variously of Christmas cake, honey, Nan's home-made meat pie, pear cider, creamed rice, Bakewell tarts, Ribena, port and Glacier mints, with an undercurrent of roast turkey. It's what I imagined ambrosia might taste like, or the nectar of the gods. "Ohh, it's…wow," I gurgled like a toddler. "What is this? It's sweet, and it's savoury; it's soothing. It's really quite…zzzzz."

"Soporific?" Pete said softly. He smiled as he scooped me off the floor and laid me out on the bed.

Day 18. *I woke up somewhere different, somewhere completely unfamiliar. It was a luxury penthouse, very bright and modern. "I won't be long," said a woman's voice. I caught a glimpse of the back of her naked body in the en suite bathroom. She was tall and slim with a mane of blonde hair. Was it Freeje? I couldn't be sure. I pulled off the blanket to find that I was stark naked too. On the floor was some very scanty female underwear, not much bigger than dental floss, and a pair of shoes with six inch heels.*

An empty bottle of Krystal champagne sat on the bedside table next to an expensive looking Jaeger LeCoultre watch, an open wrap of white powder and some condoms. Un-opened so...we hadn't, presumably. I couldn't remember. The windows were huge. I sat up. We were by the Thames, south side. Very posh. How did I get here?

Sinking back in the bed, I cleared my mind of all conscious thought, letting my subconscious mind take over. This technique works best in a floatation tank I'm told, but I'd used in the past to unearth memories and it tended to work. By the time the bomb had gone off, I had managed to recall most of it.

Day 15 Theo Jinnee tutted as he saw himself in the mirror. He was paunchy, his rough leathery skin was looking redder than an SWP banner and he'd have to get those horns trimmed. Luckily, in this reality, only Theo could see himself as he really was. In most other worlds he looked more like the handsome red-headed shape-changing trickster Loki, which is pronounced Loak-ee, not Lock-ee, and which had been his favourite alias for centuries.

Whispers of the "second coming" had brought him back to earth, and he had immediately detected the presence of a being of such kind-hearted innocence that it had made him physically sick. Thomas Scrimshaw was truthful, caring, polite and naïve. Everything he hated. Theo realised immediately that the boy had to be broken, and what a great pleasure it would be to do so. Having gained the kid's trust he now had him exactly where he wanted him.

Theo couldn't enter 22 Lupino Lane for obvious reasons, but he could still infiltrate the boy's dreams. He clicked his fingers and a three dimensional chess board materialised. Then he made his move. Loki was feeling lucky…

***

Dawn was breaking over New Cross when the three friends arrived. Matt, Mark and Keziah had realised that the only way to work out where Tom had gone was to get inside his head and figure out what he was thinking. "If we can recreate his escape route, maybe we'll be able to deduce where he is heading," Mark had reasoned, which is why they had left their Bermondsey hideaway at 5am and traced Thomas's journey from the court to the Elephant & Castle bus stop – documented in the *Daily Star* exclusive 'Sex-bomb Scrimbo raped me with his eyes' says bus-stop Barbie – and on to the bus that took them on to the market, the location of his last known sighting.

"This is pointless," Matty complained. "How can we know where he went next and why?"

"We're doing the right thing," Kez countered. "Don't ask me how I know, I can just feel it. If we can just retrace his steps and see what he's seen…"

"Let's all stop yapping and just concentrate," said Mark. "Think. Has anything odd happened to any of us?"

"Other than being painted as humongous terrorist scumbags?" Matt chortled.

"I had a really weird dream last night," Keziah said slowly.

"Another one?"

"Go on."

"Well it was just a man singing 'The Lambeth Walk' over and over again."

"And?"

"He was wearing a bowler hat with feathers in it."

"Lambeth again!" said Matt. "But that's in the opposite direction. We need to cross the road and go back into town."

"Right listen," Mark commanded. "Everyone hold hands and think," he said sharply.

"What is this, a séance?"

"Ssssh."

Mark shut his eyes tight. After five minutes he opened them again. "Now that's weird…"

"What is?"

"I just visualised something strange. It was a Music Hall stage, with two small ducks waddling across it, and they started doing the Lambeth Walk."

"What the ducks did?"

"You're not supposed to eat the worm in the Tequila," laughed Matty.

"Shhh," said Kez.

"That's just random shit," Matty went on. "It's just a mash-up of all the things we've dreamt about yesterday. It doesn't mean anything."

"Unless it does," Mark said slowly.

"Can I help you?" The stranger dismounted his Vespa scooter. He was tall, he wore an old t-shirt boasting 'The Who – I Can See For Miles' and spoke in an antiquated Cockney accent.

"No ta, pal." Matty snapped. Keziah put a hand on his arm to shut him up. "We're trying to figure out a riddle," she smiled.

"Crikey. Do tell."

"It's a game we're playing," Kez explained. "We have clues that we're trying to put together. There's the old song 'The Lambeth Walk, two ducks and…"

"And a music hall stage," said Mark.

"Very cryptic," the man replied. "Unless you have a little local knowledge. Do you young urchins happen to know who performed 'The Lambeth Walk'? No? Well it was a marvellous chap from Hackney called Henry Lupino who took the stage name Lupino Lane."

"So?" said Matt sulkily.

"So Lupino Lane is also the name of a road not half a mile from here."

"And the ducks?" asked Mark.

"Oh come on, didn't your old girls ever take you to bingo?"

"Two little ducks…22!" Matt smiled triumphantly.

"That's your puzzle solved," beamed the stranger.

"Do you think?"

"I know."

The rising sun behind the stranger's head had a weird halo effect.

"Thank you so much," said Keziah. "Mister?"

"Peter," he replied. "But they call me The Saint." He bowed slightly, then said "Miss?" as he ushered her to one side. "Take this," he said softly. "It's unregistered and untraceable. If you get separated from your friends you must use it."

"To phone you?"

"Good heavens , no. You know who and you'll know the number."

Keziah looked confused. "Don't worry," he went on. "It will all come good if you stay strong." He winked and added "And be lucky."

He steered her back towards the others. "God speed your great odyssey," he said warmly. "And remember 'suaviter in modo, fortiter in re'."

"Eh?" three confused hunters said as one.

"Do schools not teach Latin now? It means gentle in manner, strong in deeds. It's how the Management likes us to be."

Dizzy Detour

Day 15   I couldn't recall exactly how I'd got here, although I knew where I was. I was in the corridor that Peter had warned me not to go down alone; which meant that I must be near Freeje's room. Hmm. Maybe I'd just have a quick nose around and then pretend to just bump into her. I wouldn't want her to think I was stalking her…

The corridor was as long as one you might see in a Las Vegas hotel with just as many doors. The first one on the right had a sign on it that read: 'For One Day Only! The Thomas Scrimshaw

Story!' What? This I had to see. I turned the door knob and stepped in.

***

MATT, Mark and Keziah had only walked a couple of hundred yards when two cars screeched up onto the pavement either side of them. The first was an Audi which spilled out Watts and Sneed, the two idiot cops from Tommy's trial. The second vehicle, a Mitsubishi, contained three plain clothes officers.

"Stop where you are," shouted a thin-lipped man who flashed a warrant card. "I am Detective Sergeant Lobon and you three are under arrest."

Just looking at him made Keziah feel a chill. Lobon projected menace like a skunk projects stink.

"For what?" she said, trying to sound as defiant as possible.

"Seditious conspiracy, my dear," answered the other man whom she recognised as DI Arnott. "Cuff her Marsden."

"What's her Marsden?" sniggered Watts under his breath.

The hard-faced female detective moved towards Kez, who side-stepped and watched her slip on a recently deposited dog turd, falling face down into a second one.

"Come on!" shouted Matt, who led the charge away from the detectives. Sgt Watts stood forward to block him, confident his hefty gut would render him as unmovable as The Blob from the comic books. Matt just charged straight at him taking him and Sneed down like uniformed skittles.

The three teens ran at full pelt down Erlanger Road. The five considerably less fit cops were falling behind them but police sirens were getting closer. Seeing two more officers ahead of them, Kez took the first left and realised too late that it was a crescent bringing them back to the same road.

"So much for Lady Luck," muttered Mark.

They had two cops ahead of them and maybe a dozen behind. They were trapped; outnumbered and out-manoeuvred. Hopelessly doomed. When BLAM! A clapped-out old white van roared past the pair of uniformed Plod and executed a high speed u turn, pulling up alongside them. The passenger door flew open. "Jump in quick," said a handsome stranger. They did without question. The mystery driver slammed his pedal to the metal and roared straight at the two cops who leapt clear.

"Ace," said Mark.

"Blinding," Matt added.

"Umm, who are you?" asked Keziah.

"I'm Harry," he said, pushing back out into the New Cross traffic. "I work with Matty's uncles, Butch and Bernie. They asked me to keep an eye on you and here I am."

His eyes were as blue as the Maldives.

"What do you do for me uncles?" asked Matty, who had just noticed the 9mm Glock pistol resting on their saviour's lap.

"From the Ned Kelly in Rotherhithe, known them for years…"

"They've never mentioned you."

"No-one does, for the very good reason that officially I don't exist; no income tax, no VAT," he smiled, quoting Del-Boy, and then adding the cryptic explanation. "I'm a specialist, I make problems go away."

"Kindov like our avenging angel," Kez smiled.

"You could say that," he said. "But 'angel' might be stronging it, sweetheart…"

***

You will have seen better rooms. It was painted all over in a grim industrial grey and felt chilly even though the temperature must have been around 10oC. There was a constant high-tech hum in the background that nagged like a bad tooth, and everywhere was bathed in a cold fluorescent light which meant there was no way of telling whether it was night or day.

When the two men came in, the room felt even colder. They didn't seem to notice me at all. It was as if I wasn't really there – or maybe they weren't. The first man was a smartly dressed, bespectacled geek in a hand-made pinstriped suit. He wore a shirt and tie, and brothel-creeper shoes, which gave him the look of a particularly dorky spiv. His red hair had started to recede, but he had the kind of smile that could sell used snuff and there was a hard glint in his eyes. In one hand he was clutching a shabby brown pilot's flight-case; in the other he held a heavy chain, which was attached to a cast-iron shackle around the second man's neck.

The other man was crawling on all fours. He was a grotesque caricature of a human being. His face was fatter and shaped like a crescent moon. His jaw was his most prominent feature. It must have been five inches long and four inches across. Any bigger and he could host skiing events on it.

Both were Yanks, but the smaller chained one was dressed like a Punch from an English seaside show. One minute he was crouching, his long arms clutching his knees, the next he was leaping to his feet, thrashing his rubber limbs about and cackling obscenely. All the time crouching, leaping, crouching, leaping, like some human jack-in-the-box, until the taller man SNAPPED.

"For Pete's sake, cut it out!" he bellowed in an accent that was half smart Manhattan and half betraying his humble Indianapolis origins. "If hooters were brains you'd have the cleavage of a surfboard."

"Sorry, sorry," the Punch-like man said breathlessly as he steadied himself on his feet.

"With a walk like that you ought to be in West Hollywood."

"Yeah, sorry. It's just been so long since I've been...out."

"You've been out more times than the gas, asshole," the suited man roared. "Out of luck, out of chokey, out of time...and then back in to the freakin' Cuckoo's Nest where you belong. In, out, in, out, you're the original Okey Cokey man."

"Well it feels like forever," the Punch man declared in his chirping New England staccato. "It feels like I've been left on the shelf."

"Humph," grunted the tall, skinny man. "Dog meat's got a long shelf-life."

"PEDIGREE CHUM! Top breeders recommend it!" yelped the fool, who proceeded to bark like an enraged Chihuahua."

His companion sighed. "Honestly, talking to you is like trying to teach algebra to a garden gnome." He looked around the room and elaborately pursed his lips. "Jeez," he said. "This place. They've got morgues in Bosnia that are more inviting than this. Hey, butt-breath, know any horror stories? They'd sure go with the atmosphere."

"What do ghosts wear on their feet? BOOOOOOOTS! Geddit? BOOOOOOOTS."

"Can it, chump," the taller man growled. "Y'know, you're a real ignoranus."

"The word is ignoramus," said the chained man with dignity.

"Not in your case, as you're both dumb and an asshole. You sir are about as much use as a garlic mouthwash."

The Punch looked at his feet, forlornly.

"Look at ya," the taller, suited man continued. "You look like an explosion in the Libertines' dressing room." He shook his head. "How did I get involved in all this, a man of my calibre? I should be interviewing Rihanna, not baby-sitting some over-grown weasel."

"Just as long as you don't host the Academy Awards again," smirked the Punch.

"Hey!"

"I hear you're emigrating to Australia just so you can watch your career go down the plughole in the opposite direction."

"Why you...."

"Take it easy, mind your heart, old chum. In fact..." the chained man began to sing, "Hit the Prozac, and don't you come back no more, no more, no more, no more..."

The taller man shot him a look he could have shaved with. "C'mon," he said. "Let's get this over with."

He stepped forward and ripped open his shirt to reveal a Superman-like costume underneath, but with a giant L where the S should be. He reached into his flight bag and produced a chair and then a large desk, far bigger than the bag itself and sat behind it. Then out came an old-fashioned phone, an even more old-fashioned microphone and a stack of cue cards. Finally he pulled out a DVD disc, which he gave to the smaller chained man. "Put this in the machine and let's get ready to start," he ordered.

"No," the fool replied. "Look, this is episode two. We've halfway into the story."

"Damn," the taller man snapped. Then he looked straight out of this page and into your eyes, and hollered: "You WEASEL! You've started without us. That is totally against regulations here at the Ed Sullivan Theatre. It means everyone joining us now will need an update from this joker..."

The smaller man bowed theatrically, his giant chin scraping the floor.

"OK, can it," groaned his companion, who gave an ironic wink to an unseen camera then went on. "I'd better fill you in. My name is Letterman, a regular late night comedy superhero armed with unfeasibly sharp one-liners, put downs and a kinda left-field way of looking at the world. And this clown is my so-called rival Jay The Joker, the perpetual motion human joke machine who gets his strength from straight-forward joshin', topical gags and his general JACKASS amiability."

The machine clicked. "Are we set?"

Jay nodded.

"OK folks," Letterman continued. "It's show time! And just as shit comes before the shovel, so, unlikely as it seems, only one guy can set the scene for you – it's just tough luck that it has to be this reject from Magneto's brotherhood of evil mutants...man, this guy is uglier than a bucket full of butts."

"Listen to him," Jay sighed. "You'll be hearing a lot about this guy here soon, folks. Oh yeah, he'll be big news one day. I hear he smokes in bed."

"Oh now you're funny," Letterman countered. "All this chapter without a laugh and now you start?" He fiddled with his cue cards, cleared his throat theatrically and then announced: "Folks, I give you a man more cracked than a public bar urinal and just as glamorous, Jayyyyyy Lenoman!"

With these words, Letterman slipped Lenoman off his chain and Jay sprang to his feet and began to cavort wildly, flinging his flimsy body around the room, bouncing off the walls and ceiling like a loco pin-ball. At one point he went straight through me without either of us feeling a thing. Finally he grew tired of this sport, stopped and bowed low into an imaginary spotlight.

"Welcome folks," he said. "Thank you for coming. This odd odyssey, this rebel yelp, is the true story of Thomas Scrimshaw. He's just seventeen and completely oblivious to the fact that he is tottering on the verge of interstellar stardom. Thomas was born in Woolwich, South East London on the great ape planet earth in 1997.

"I wouldn't say it was a rough area, but the neighbourhood Samaritans were a front for the Yardies and the local vicar sold the choirboys glue.

"Thomas's mom was kind and considerate, but a slight woman. His father was also a slight woman having a suspect chromosome balance. He'd spent four years attached to Barclay's Bank in India. Fortunately important men from the British Embassy came and cut him down.

"Thomas had a poor but pleasant upbringing. His home-life was so happy that they had to go somewhere miserable for holidays just to have a break. Usually Great Yarmouth. His parents were fussy and over-protective. His mom was so house-proud that she banned Thomas's pals from visiting him and as she rarely let him out at nights, the lad tended to withdraw into himself... an amazing contortion in which the most prominent parts of his body were reversed inwards, beginning with his buttocks and ending with his nose. This made breathing difficult but it did explain how he came to talk out of the back of his head so often."

Letterman slapped the desk violently at this absurdity and gobbed into a spittoon.

Lenoman carried on regardless. "The only thing that kept Thomas going was noise, his God-awful collection of racket-mongers, groups like Nirvana, Rancid and Five Finger Death Punch. Iron Maiden was his first love, a right evil crew of ear-splitters. Under their influence, Thomas started to take guitar lessons but he took to musicianship like a jackass takes to jet-skiing. So he never did become the leather-clad Lothario of his lucid imagination. He was genuinely in love with life, though, and that's how things remained until life jilted him with one almighty kick in the gonads."

Letterman had had enough. "What are you on, fella?" he roared. "You're going all over the place like an over-caffeinated monkey. Just tell the god-damn story."

"Give me a chance."

"Go slam your dick in the door. Girls were the problem, right? This kid couldn't get laid with a pocket full of pardons in a woman's penitentiary."

"That's about the size of it," Jay agreed. "And the size of it was also a worry but we won't pry. Little Tommy had no females in his family his own age and unbeknown to him his shyness around girls was a by-product of his undiagnosed Asperger's. His parents' divorce knocked him deeper into himself. He didn't mix with any at school. He led a very sheltered life..."

"What d'you mean sheltered? Did he spend the first six years under some giant canvas construction in the art room, or what?"

"He might as well have done. When the other kids were out clubbing, Thomas was chess clubbing. He was sad. How sad, you ask? So sad he got aroused by rugby song lyrics and Jessica Rabbit.

"Sad? The nearest he ever came to an erotic experience was phoning up the speaking clock to hear the operator say 'on the third stroke'..."

An unseen drummer hit a rim-shot. "Sad? He went to the local massage parlour and it was self-service." Another rim-shot.

"Sad? The one time he'd turned on the local sex symbol was when he plugged in the flashing condom sign at the neighbourhood drug store..."

Letterman whipped out a Double Tap 9mm and shot the drummer. "Was he ever sexually confused?" he asked.

"When he was 15 he started wearing a 32-inch bra, but he soon grew out of it. Then, last summer his luck changed. He stumbled into an office job and he met her, his first romantic obsession – Freeje, a mysterious untamed rock chick. But then through a series of preordained disasters he lost the job, got arrested, broke out of custody and is on the run. And that is where we find him now."

"And is he happy?"

"Of course he's not. He's a wanted man! And wanted by the cops, not the woman! Life to Thomas seems about as frustrating as flying to the moon and finding you've left the landing ladder at home."

"And what about these weird experiences I hear he's having?"

"I don't know about them, I haven't watched episode one yet."

"Asshole."

"Asshole? Me? I've just done the monologue for you and all you can say is I'm an asshole?"

"You're right. I'm sorry. You're a fuggin' asshole."

Letterman clipped Jay sharply around the ears, sending him flying.

I'd seen enough, and returned to the corridor. There was a sign on the wall with an arrow pointing to right and the words 'This Way Thomas'. Some unseen benefactor was clearly trying to help me.

Back in the room, Lenoman was glaring at his attacker. "Jesus, why did you do that?" he said, rubbing his arm. "You could have given me a clap. I always say a little clap is better than a lot of herp."

"Do you want to see your nuts fly out of your nose, asshole?"

"Not really. Not unless it gets me a slot on America's Got Talent."

"So okay, let's get this straight. This story we're relating is like Gulliver's Travels only instead of Gulliver we get a gormless kid who is clearly on the spectrum. Is that right?"

"More like Gullible's Troubles, I'd say."

"So what happens next?"

"We can't be sure, but we do know the choices Thomas makes in the next 24 hours will seal mankind's fate for a millennium."

"Jeez, you'd better play the god-damn DVD then."

Grumbling under his breath, Jay bounced over to the far wall and quickly stripped away its surface like wet wallpaper to uncover a gigantic cinema screen. He then returned to the machine and pressed play.

Letterman looked up at you, the reader and barked sternly: "Sit up straight! Stop slouching! We'll catch with you after these messages from our sponsors. See you at the start of episode three, OK? No flipping."

(The adverts that followed would only make sense to inhabitants of the planet Minge, six trillion light years from earth. For the benefit of human readers, they have been cut from this edition of the book.)

***

The next three doors were close together, two on the right and one on the left. Their signs were equally intriguing, they said 'Thomas gets rich', 'Thomas finds fame' and 'Thomas gets the girl'. I hesitated outside that last one for a moment. From inside a woman's voice said "Come" so seductively I nearly did. But for some reason at the last minute I changed my mind.

***

Harry dropped off the gang at the Bermondsey safe-house, with stern warnings not to venture out again until night time. Not a single one of them had noticed him slip a small electronic tracking device into Keziah's bag, and neither had they heard him say the words "Seagull is tagged, repeat Seagull is tagged' as he drove away.

"He was so fit," she said dreamily.

"Now, now, Tommy will be jealous," Matt laughed.

"Pig!"

"You really knocked those cops for six earlier Matt," said Mark. "It was pretty remarkable."

"It felt a bit strange now I think about it," he replied. "Almost like I'd turned into something more than me..."

"Like The Bull?"

"Yeah, I guess so."

"And Keziah's awesome good fortune came into play too didn't it, with the dog shit, and then Harry turning up. Could be a coincidence, but…"

"Are you suggesting we're becoming superheroes for real?"

"Well maybe you two, but nothing's happened to me yet."

"It's just adrenalin and chance," scoffed Keziah. "Let's not get ahead of ourselves. At least now we're here we can use a laptop to plan our route. If we leave here around 8pm we can make it to Lupino Lane by 10. Maybe walk apart but in sight of each other."

"Let's check out the wardrobes upstairs," said Matt. "They're bound to be full of cloths we can adapt."

"What is it your uncles do exactly, Matt?"

"Oh, a little bit of this, a little bit of that…"

***

Theo Jinnee chose his moment perfectly; making his move on his 3D board game at precisely the moment that Thomas reached the three doors. He picked up a piece and laid it on its side. Thomas passed out immediately, but in his dream world he would be exactly the same place, facing exactly the same temptations. Temptations Theo could now influence, temptations as old as recorded history. Temptations that could potentially change the future of the planet – money, fame and sex. What would goody two-shoes sell his soul for he wondered? He didn't think the idealistic young socialist would be swayed by spondoolicks. Sex? Maybe. He'd turned the lovely Lucy down in the courthouse but then there the boy was making his escape at the time. She would still be of use undermining his defences. She'd be his Trojan horse. Or more precisely his Trojan pussy…But Theo was certain Thomas would go for fame above all else; the smart ones always did, because when you have that the sex and money comes to you anyway. He could justify fame in his head by arguing he could use celebrity status to further good causes. And then he'd sell out like everyone else he'd pursued over the centuries, all the so-called great and good. Lincoln, Castro, Mother Theresa…they weren't all that. Blair was the easiest one to turn; Scrimshaw would be child's play. The world was about to change, he could smell it. Tomorrow belonged to him.

Day 16. Inspector Arnott was happy. Thanks to his first class U/C operative he could now keep tabs on the Smith girl and her two yobbo accomplices. And thanks to his hard-working director of press, he could rely on regular headline scare stories about the three which he was convinced would radically accelerate the cops' news agenda.

Today's *Mail* had an exclusive on the evil goals of the Scrimbonistas which purported to list the 'criminal targets' masterminded by Thomas's three teenage lieutenants as they built up a network of radical anarchists cells throughout the land. These targets apparently included Harrods, Kings Road Chelsea and the Brent Cross Shopping Centre where an incendiary device would 'strike a decisive blow against consumer capitalism'. The paper's editorial accused Scrimshaw and his gang of becoming a beacon for the nation's disaffected youth. It also carried a hefty two and a bit page article by the Conservative historian Dominic Sandbrook on how the Scrimbonistas with their treasonous sedition were taking their cue from 19th Century Russian anarchists, the Latvian George Gardstein and the followers of Kropotkin.

The cumulative effect would, Arnott felt, would make the trio panic and drive them to regroup with their evil mastermind cult leader Thomas Scrimshaw as soon as possible – and the Met's finest would be right there when they did, Tasered up and ready to take them down.

***

Have you ever wondered what the Devil sings when the mood takes him? A few miles away a house in New Cross reverberated with a rich baritone rendition of The Sheik of Araby … "Each night before she sleeps – with no pants on – into her tent he creeps – with no pants on…" Well you didn't expect him to have good taste, did you? Theo Jinnee was chuffed because he had Thomas Scrimshaw exactly where he wanted him. He walked into his office beaming and sat at his lower desk. The office was two-tier, a seductive mix of antiquity and modernity. The downstairs half, its walls ingrained with hashish and opium, was crammed with what some would call false idols, the gods of a hundred religions depicted in wood, bronze, gold and bone; upstairs looked more like a 1990s sci-fi director's idea of a 22nd Century workplace, a minimalist temple of light with changing wall panels and a floating bank of plasma screens which constituted a more rudimentary but fully operational version of the Eye of Horus.

The Jinnee sipped absinthe from a pint pot and grinned. His good mood lasted until the moment he glanced at the morning's headlines, realised what Scotland Yard were up to and scowled. The last thing he wanted was for Thomas to be tracked down by any pesky pals who would wake him from his dreams and influence his decisions.

Theo had people in the Met of course, but this case was too high profile for them to intervene. They'd be under too much scrutiny. No, he'd have to deploy other forces to stall the troublesome teens. He knew exactly who.

Roads To Nowhere

Part One: The Gangs of New Cross

Joey Bishop smiled when he took the call. He beat people up for fun, getting paid for it was a bonus. And when the pictures of the three targets came through on his iPhone his smile turned into a chuckle. He'd had a run-in with these scumbags before – proper lefties, Paki-lovers, probably pansies. This was going to be a pleasure.

***

The rain hit South London like a torrent. Matt, Mark and Keziah sheltered under an oak tree in Southwark Park, questioning their decision to make the three mile journey back to New Cross on foot. Matty felt it would be safer than risking public transport, and so they had left the safe-house at 11pm and set off walking twenty paces apart – the cops and the media would be looking for a gang of three. The downpour had started five or six minutes later.

"It's like a monsoon," moaned Matty.

"The gutters are over-flowing," said Keziah. "Have you ever known rain like this?"

"Never," said Mark.

"It's like Thor's taking a piss," smiled Matty. Thunder immediately erupted.

"That's spooky."

The lightening came three seconds later.

"It's getting closer," said Kez. "It's probably not the best time to be sheltering under a tree. Shall we...oh shit."

"What?" asked Mark.

"Behind you. It's Joey Bishop. And he's brought his mates from Planet Ugly."

"One piece of crap even this rain won't flush away," observed Matty.

Bishop was firm-handed. He'd brought his brothers, his gang and his dad who carried an ornate cane. Twelve in total, a dirty dozen dead-beat boneheads all brimful of malice and getting closer by the second.

"Oi, wankers!" Bishop yelled pleasantly. "You're on our manor now, and I am gonna fuck ya good and proper – especially you baby." He pointed at Keziah and grabbed his crotch. "I've got something here that's big enough to even fill your trap."

"Well it certainly isn't his IQ," she muttered. Matty looked at them. "I'm not having this, I'm going in."

Shoulder down Matty charged the gang's left flank scattering them like ten-pins and yelling "Strike!" like a regular comic book hero. His triumph didn't last long. Joey's firm recovered rapidly and five of them jumped him, leaving Bishop, his dad and his brothers to turn on Kez and Mark.

The three brothers formed a semi-circle around Mark, while their father leered at Keziah. He was wearing a Millwall shirt and Slazenger trainers but his gut suggested it had been a decade or two since he'd scored – in any sense. The old man lunged at her but she managed to trip him into falling face first in the mud.

Another one of the gang ran at her from the right; she took him down with a sweeping hip throw. Kez smiled, her luck was holding. But sadly not for long. Bishop Senior used his cane to trip her and then pulled a sword from inside it.

"Don't top it yet, pop," shouted Joey. "I'm gonna podger that one first."

He and his brothers kept coming at Mark. Mark was a decent boxer but he couldn't guard against punches from three directions. The brothers rained heavy blows on him and they were hurting. In desperation Mark grabbed Joey by the ears and stared into his eyes intently before losing consciousness.

Matty had just finished smashing the last of his attackers into the ground when he turned and saw Mark and Joey pass out. Worse he saw Bishop's brothers turn towards Keziah undoing theirs Levis while the old bastard towered over her with a sword in his hand. Shit. He started to run at them but he slipped and fell.

Keziah glared at Joey as he pulled himself off the floor. "Me first," he told his brothers – Tweedledum and Tweedledumber, she thought. His father raised the sword above his head to intimidate her. Big mistake. Above them the thunder roared and a bolt of lightning struck him killing his instantly. Mark who had regained consciousness was looking on in utter confusion. Grief-stricken the brothers went for Kez only for Joey to rabbit punch the biggest one. While he went down in agony, Matty smashed the other bruv brother into unconsciousness. "Your turn now," he said to Joey.

"Hang on mate," Bishop replied. "It's me Matt, it's Mark. I did it. Somehow I took over this bastard's body. Hold on, watch…"

He turned towards his own body and stared. Mark instantly snapped wide awake as Joey Bishop hit the deck.

"How about that?" Mark grinned.

"Poor Kez never got to bed the Bishop after all then."

"No-one even got to bash the bishop," Mark replied.

"My disappointment is palpable," said Kez. "But at least we now know we all seem to have acquired strange abilities…Three is a magic number all right."

"Talking of which, nice work with the lightning by the way," said Matt.

"Oh I can't take the credit for that," Kez replied, smiling enigmatically and choosing not to mention the face of the thunder god who had smiled at her after the old scumbag copped it.

Thor's storm fizzled out to a fine rain, as the three amigos walked on leaving behind eleven unconscious yobbos and one Kentucky fried corpse.

***

The three, still walking apart, reached St Mary's church when their next obstacle appeared, a twenty strong gang of Peckham boys swaggered towards them. Matty spotted them first and pointed into the graveyard to regroup. This wasn't going to be as easy. Most of the gang carried knives and machetes but one youth had an assault rifle.

"That's an AK74," said Mark.

"Not a 47?" asked Matty.

"No, it's smaller. Russian, from the 70s."

"Spare me the geek insights, either way we're screwed," said Kez. "It's going to take more than a bit of luck, a bit of body-swopping and a raging bull charge to stop this lot."

"Oh swopping, I was thinking of challenging them to some body-popping…"

"Not now, Mark."

The youth with the gun discharged it, blasting chunks of stone off the tombstones they were sheltering behind.

"Best you bwois turn around and go back where you came from," shouted the leader whose eyebrows, Keziah noticed, resembled chunky caterpillars. Little did she know he had already made Tom's acquaintance. "Ya get me? Before me blads lose patience. Dis is my yard, innit?"

He then stepped forward and spoke in Cockney: "Best you turn aht yer sky-rockets before you do one, though, eh me old chinas?"

"I'm afraid we can't do that, mate," replied Mark. "Our 'blad' needs us."

He stood up planning to lock eyes and swop bodies with the gang leader, but as he did so the ground below their feet started trembling. It felt like an earthquake tremor. Matty pulled him down.

The rumbling grew stronger; the ground was shaking like a fairground rattler. And groaning – the noise was unnerving. It sounded like the earth was in pain. Worse, the sounds felt weirdly human.

Even the cockier gang members looked concerned.

With one last courage-curdling roar of agony, the soil beneath their feet started to open up and skeletons began to emerge from the consecrated ground; the remains of dockers, sailors, sweeps, lightermen and other old Cockneys somehow reanimated and moving towards the gang with chortling enthusiasm.

The kid with the AK74 let loose a few deafening rounds but bullets put no fear into those already dead. The yout' turned and ran, many discarding their weapons in panic and, some with distinct wet patches down the front of their designer jeans.

Then the skeletons turned towards the gang of three. "Oi," said one. "Git orff ov moi 'eadstone," and then he laughed heartily.

"Who…what?" Keziah started to say.

"Shut your bone box and get on yer way, townies," the fleshless corpse continued in a broad 19th century London voice. "Them bloomin' toe-rags won't bovver yous agen. Cam on, shift yer arses before the blue bottles show. Tommy needs ya so 'e do."

As quickly as they had materialised, the band of bony brothers returned to their resting place, the earth above creaking into action and sealing itself over them as if nothing at all had happened.

"How the…?"

"Don't even ask. Just thank God or whoever is responsible for that."

"We could have had 'em," moaned Matt.

"Maybe," Mark replied. "But I'm pretty glad we didn't need to. None of us is bullet-proof as far as I know."

"Yet," said Matty. "Don't forget the yet."

"We are officially team Nemesis now though."

Keziah patted the ground. "Is it too soon to say, poor old sod?" she smiled.

"Yes," they replied as one.

It was still dark when the three reached the outskirts of New Cross, unfortunately the main road was blocked. Not by the police, but by a large gang of burly denim and leather-clad Hell's Angels, all of whom appeared to be clutching cudgels, chains or machetes.

The next morning's Metro told the full story of the Southwark riot in remarkable and quite imaginative detail. Under the headline 'Chaos In The City' the free sheet reported a spree of arson and looting by armed gangs. 'Scrimbo, the baby-faced villain has gone to ground', said the editorial 'but his skinhead followers are armed, dangerous and addicted to conflict'. It called on the Chairman Mandelson to 'deploy the SAS throughout South London and end this bloody chaos'.

Roads To Nowhere Part 2

Trouble is coming, temptation

I woke up to tapering plumes of smoke above my head. I was in Theo Jinnee's office. My eccentric tramp/private eye saviour was puffing away on a six foot hookah. He seemed preoccupied with some kind of art project. Theo had laid two muslin sheets on the floor and was slowly dribbling paint over the top one.

"What do you think?" he asked me without turning around. I walked over and was surprised to see a rather good likeness of me. Jinnee pulled apart the sheets to reveal a near-identical one underneath.

"Neat, but why two?"

"To symbolize the ages-old opposites of human nature. They're not quite the same," he continued, flicking bits of paint at them.

"I'm not interested in appearance, Thomas," he said, his voice now languidly seductive. "I'm interested in essence, the mystery of inner life. With you it's an innocence so rare that it's virtually extinct; that and a quaint belief in humanity, of the perfectibility of the naturally imperfect."

One portrait had acquired a golden glow, I noticed; the other a distinct crimson aura.

"Good and evil," he said lightly. "Yin and yang….it's an illusion. You're still the same person, the same essence. Just differently inclined…"

I wanted to add right and wrong but he carried on speaking. "Art exists on a higher plain than reality, my dear boy. Art sees truth that logic does not, Art reflects the soul."

He turned and flashed me a grin that revealed nearly all of his yellowing fangs. "All I ask is why strive after the unobtainable when you could obtain the world?"

He clicked his fingers and I found myself back in the Corridor of Doors. 'Tommy Plays Smart' said the first one. I pushed it gently open and stepped in to find myself in a small cinema screening room. The image on screen was an animated version of The Three Little Pigs, frozen on their petrified pink faces. I sat down to watch and found myself next to Jinnee who was loaded up with popcorn, Pepsi Cola and Peppermint Schnapps.

"It's all about perspective, Tom," he said, continuing the same conversation. "Now, I know you know this story. You're on the side of the piglets of course, and against the Big Bad Wolf. Boo hiss etc. But tell me, can he help being Big? Of course not. That's down to his genes. And why is he bad? Because he wants to eat? What's the guy supposed to do? Starve? It's unnatural. It's propaganda! And by the way the storytellers don't tell you that when these schmucks were building their houses with straw and wood and finally stone, there was a fourth little pig building one of glass and steel. He made an absolute killing when the property market went up, too. The fourth pig was okay, these three clowns were barely worth a bacon sandwich. It's all about perspective. Now check this out."

He clicked his fingers and a different cartoon played. Now I was watching an animated me giving food parcels to the poor before getting into a chauffeur-driven Bentley.

"See, you're still a good guy but you have money," Jinnee said cheerfully. "This can happen! I can make you rich! I can make you happy" – the animation showed me with a beautiful blonde wife and two kids beaming proudly outside a deluxe modern office block that said Scrimshaw Global Enterprises PLC.

"You could have all this and afford to help the poor and the needy."

"Wow," I said simply.

"Wow indeed. You see, you could still do lots of charity work but in style. You could make things change because you'd have the resources and manpower at your finger tips to do so. And after a hard day's work, why not relax in style? After all, you're a good guy, you deserve it."

The animation moved on. I had my own box at The Valley to watch Charlton with family and friends. I entertained the old gang generously over steaming plates of corn beef hash at The Ivy, I was driven home from nightclubs by a chauffeur who looked suspiciously like my old boss Clarkson. This was fun. But then the story moved on. In the next scene, a waiter at the Chiltern Firehouse spilt champagne on my suit – "Clumsy fool!" Theo heckled, and then he laughed as I had the guy sacked.

In the following scene Clarkson the chauffeur turned up late and I gave him a humiliating public dressing down. Minutes later, I was in the back of a stretch limo groping a very willing table dancer and working my way through the kind of cocaine mountain Al Pacino enjoyed in Scarface...

"Perks, perks, perks!" shouted Jinnee triumphantly. "Revenge, riches and wanton bitches!"

"No!" I shouted. "That's not me! That will never be me!"

At that precise moment I found myself back in my bedroom.

***

Down Queen's Road from Peckham
Three heroes boldly strode
To the border where Pepys
Meets the old New Cross Road

Facing them, a human tide
A force of savagery
Bedecked in red and white
Death's Heads and imagery

Of bikes and wars and drugs
And yes of Thanatos
United they would face these thugs
Victory at any cost

Theirs not to reason why
Theirs not to sit and sigh
Theirs just to do or die
Into the valley of death
To aid fair Thomas

Matty he did make the charge
Mark took out Fat Ray's mind
While Kez did jinx those she
Could, behind enemy lines

Too many forces faced them
Too strong the enemy

It would've took King Arthur's knights
To best such pedigree

"Retreat pals," bold Matt shouted
"Retreat, regroup, re-plan"
But back safe from battle
He could not see the gang

Near through the line they broke
Hot blood their shirts did soak
Teen limbs with hearts of oak but
Driven from the mouth of hell
Alone poor Thomas

***

I was home; in bed in fact, but oddly paralyzed. I didn't appear to be strapped down but I couldn't move. Thanks Jinnee. I looked around for an escape route but couldn't physically enter the first of the three pictures I tried. Maybe that 'gift' had worn off.

Bored I looked at a glamour shot of Loaded model Connie-Lyn, 18, from Colchester. 'Connie-Lyn has been modelling ever since she left school, but dreams of a career in reality TV,' read the caption. 'She made her first small screen appearance with her foot-balling father Mike Gus at three years old and...'

Whoosh. I couldn't read any more as I'd been sucked into the picture, landing slap bang on the bed in the modelling shoot. Connie-Lyn screamed, the photographer Ross Grossenberq went potty. "What the feck are you doing?" he roared in a broad Killarney accent. "Who the feck are you and why are you in my studio?"

I thought quickly. "Tom Scrim...mington-Smythe," I said as poshly as I could manage. "Associate Producer of the new Nuts TV hidden camera show Carnal Camera. And you my delightful girl have been chosen as our first victim."

She smiled at me so sexily I'm surprised my fly didn't spontaneously burst open.

"Where are your feckin' cameras then?" asked Grossenberq with justified suspicion.

"Hidden in your studio lights," I noticed his wedding ring. "We cleared it with your other half."

"But how…"

"Never mind that, Ross," Connie-Lyn said sharply. "Why don't you run along to the coffee shop on the corner and get Mr, Scrimmy…?"

"Scrimington-Smythe," I beamed.

"Yes get Thomas a cappuccino, or…

"A Latte would be good, thanks. No, hang about, I'll have a café cubano please." That would impress her.

The photographer glowered but she waved him away.

"Now tell me, what made you pick me?"

"It was your smile," I said. "I saw one of your photo sessions and I thought this woman could light up a room."

"So have I disappointed you, in the flesh?"

"Far from it, you're…gorgeous." And she was. As curvy as a Scalextric track, with oceans of natural blonde hair and Nordic blue eyes.

"Do you think I could progress in television?" she asked, coquettishly, a finger lightly brushing my trousers.

"Oh very much so. Now having spoken to you, I realise you have the voice and the personality to be a presenter." I started to hate myself but she was sooo hot.

"I so want to be famous," she squealed.

"Why?"

"To be somebody."

"You are somebody, you already have some helluva body."

"To be in OK! Magazine."

I sighed. My scruples were kicking in.

"To be known!" she said emphatically.

"But wouldn't it be better to be known for having a special talent rather than for just being famous?"

"Are you saying these aren't special?" she asked, coquettishly pushing her ample breasts in my direction.

"Yes, but…"

"Oh I get it, don't say another word." She got up and bolted the studio door. "We need to get to know each other better." She paused and removed her bra. "Much, much better. Now, let me show you my other special talent…"

My groin said yes, but yet again my stupid bloody conscience needed to think about it.

"Why don't I take you for a meal tonight?" I said. "I'll give you one of my cards."

"Not shy are you Thomas?" she said teasingly, the finger now finding the, umm, root of my indecision.

"Worse," I said solemnly. "Moral."

And that was it. I was back in Theo's office.

***

The battle with the Hell's Angels had been fierce and brutal. Matty had been heroic, taking out at least thirty of the chain-wielding bikers single-handedly, while Mark's body-hopping had caused chaos and confusion and led to bitter inter-gang rucks. Unfortunately there had been so many "greasers" that the three had got separated. Keziah had used her charms to avoid injury but now she couldn't see either of the boys.

Kez shivered in the wind, like a solitary leaf. Maybe Lady Luck's luck had finally run out.

More gangs were assembling in both directions – Road Rats, punks, psychobillies, Mods, Millwall Bushwhackers…What to do?

She turned down a side road looking for a back garden to hide in. At the far end she noticed a small church. Sanctuary she thought, remembering the Iron Maiden song rather than her history lessons, 'sanctuary from the law'.

***

Beware the Jinnee, Tom old son
His bark and yes his bite
He's lured you in and had his fun

138

And now the end's in sight

"I'm very pleased with you Thomas," the man I still thought of as my friend said, with a smile that would have dazzled an Osmond. "You have been tested and you've proved to be strong…You've rejected the temptations of sex and money, and only the purest of hearts could do that."

"Who are you Mr Jinnee?"

"Theo please."

"You're not who you say you are, are you?"

"Very astute, my boy. No I am not. It's time for transparency…"

Theo's face began to quiver as it morphed and his body grew. His skin grew redder, his ears enlarged. So did he. He was ten foot tall now.

"I'm not Theo. I am The Jinnee, known to your ancestors as Loki. And to some as…"

"The Devil."

"Yeah, what can I say? I've had a bad press. They say I'm a force for evil, but I have brought a sense of playfulness to the world. Who do you think is responsible for Boris Johnson? Who made George W the American President or John Prescott Deputy Leader of the Labour Party? Who persuaded George Galloway to go on Celebrity Big Brother and pretend to be a cat? Moi, moi, moi…

"That was one of my greatest ruses – up there were disco music, train timetables and 'Call Waiting'. And wait for my next trick. I'm working on Donald Trump running for the White House. Ridiculous? Yes. Hilarious of course. He might even win!

"Robert Maxwell was mine, ego the size of the Holyland Tower! Icke –
ICKE! – as mad as a box of frogs!" He roared with laughter.

"I'm a god of mischief, not evil. I'm a fun guy, Tom! You've seen a taste of their heaven at Lupino Lane. Ballroom dances and cream teas! Dull or what? And wait till you get to the real joint – the lobby is like a Morrisons supermarket goods entrance. You go in like a delivery of dog food! If that's all the after-life has to offer it's a wonder man bothered to crawl out of the sea in the first place. At my place, which I'd *luhhve* you to visit, we have clubs devoted to punk, rock, extreme metal, Ska, jazz and funk."

He clicked his fingers and the heady whirl of Patrick Hernandez's Born To Be Alive exploded forcefully out of unseen speakers as party scenes flashed before my eyes.

"Champagne comes out of the taps!" he said excitedly. "We had an orgy once that lasted for 927 years. It only stopped when that killjoy Stalin turned up. The only 'fires of Hell' are our smoking barbecue rib pits serving up honey-roasted boar and spice-packed bangers 24/7. As for the women, it's party central! Anything a body desires is there for the taking. You should come."

The visions vanished.

"Yeah, maybe one day. When I've sorted out the mess my life is in."

"Well, now, you see, I could sort all that out for you...but, hey, I realise you don't entirely trust me and I can understand why. Centuries of right-wing Christian propaganda are going to leave their mark. And I've seen for myself that you are above the temptations of the flesh. But let me say this, who has been your friend on this whole journey so far? Who has helped you on every occasion? That's right, soppy old Satan, that's who. Me, Lucifer! I've been your biggest supporter. And what I can do, with no strings right now, is help reinvent you."

"I, erh..."

"No, don't be too hasty. Listen. If you were famous, you'd have a platform. If you were famous, people would listen to you. If you were famous, you could clear your name and spread your message. Or His one. And only you can do that because you see the thing about my old mate Yahwah, or Jehovah or whatever he calls himself these days is he's never been a realist. Take this sin business. It's so easy for people to sin, so much in human nature that the only way you could be sure of avoiding it is to kill yourself which of course is another sin. So is it any wonder so many holy Joes go mental?

"God isn't so great, my friend. He plays tricks on humanity all the time. Think about it. If you take Christianity at face value there are only a few conclusions about your God you can come to. Either he is willing to prevent evil but not able, in which case he's not Almighty at all. Or he is able but not willing, in which case he's surely pretty evil himself. And if he is willing and able why does evil exist? To test and torment you! What are you, his toys? His playthings?"

"I never looked at it like that."

"Mani back in the third century saw the material world as my creation. Marriage and procreation were grave sins since by having kids people create more sinners to multiply my work…and consequently his preferred solution was to move mankind to the super-terrestrial realm of Good and Light by way of gradual extinction, something that the West seems to have adopted judging by your demographic suicide, but I digress.

"You, Tom, are important because you have the same purity of the soul as him and the same ideals as he does…"

"As God?"

"Yes, but you're more of a realist."

Theo put his arm around my shoulder, giving me a whiff of his strange sulphurous aftershave and continued. "You can see the flaws that the big man can't, and so you are better placed to sell them to your fellow man. All you need is fame. Now I know you'll say your picture has been seen enough but what you have now is infamy, and what you need is some serious rebranding."

"Aren't you over-looking the minor inconvenience of me being Public Enemy number one?"

"But say I can prove your innocence!" he snapped back, his eyes burning with the fire of inspiration. "Unseen CCTV evidence, new eye-witness testimonies, a clean bill of health from MI5 and the CIA…all of that is a piece of cake.

"Listen, here's the plan Stan. I assemble all that and you appeal your sentence in the European Court of Justice, which I control. You will win. There will be a huge PR campaign on your behalf. There will be public apologies from Mandelson down. You'll do a big televised interview with someone the public detests, like Piers Morgan, and you'll tell your side of the story. There will be a best-selling autobiography and, being you, you'll give all the proceeds to charity. I played that song of yours…"

"The Laughing Weasel, how…?"

"Yes. That's the one. I played it to Calvin Harris. He's already remixed it into a monster. My good friend Simon Cowell will release it. You'll fly to Number One like shit off a shovel. You'll have to pretend to date Taylor Swift for a week and at the height of all that you will become Britain's best-loved celebrity. Your re-birth will be complete. Infamy will become fame. You'll go from conspirator to national treasure, from devil to angel – and not for personal gain but to further the cause of the Lord…"

"But why would you do that for me? You hate God."

"Yes I do, but I know when I'm beaten. Like that other one, the carpenter's son, you are incorruptible. Believe me I've tried. You have rejected money, you rejected the pleasures of the flesh…To misquote Monty Python, you're not a very naughty boy, you're the Messiah."

"If I had a platform I could explain that everything people think they know about me is wrong."

"You could."

"I could clear my name."

"Yes. Justice would out!"

"I could spread a message of peace and love."

"You could. That's what comes from the hallowed world of celebrity today: an audience, followers. It's a megaphone to the masses. You can become a celeb without compromising. Look…into your future…"

Theo waved his hand and the wall became a bank of TV screens showing various scenarios – me on TV, me headlining Wembley with a backing band, me helping the homeless, my Mum beaming with pride, and just a quick flash of me walking down the aisle with a blonde. It wasn't clear who it was from the rear view…

"Wow. And all I'd have to do…"

"Is sign this no-strings management contract."

Theo produced a stack of legal papers from nowhere with an antique quilted pen and placed both in my hands.

"I need to study the small print."

"Of course you must! You're no mug."

"No, I'm not."

"You've been through enough. You won't get fooled again. Here, drink this."

He poured a large glass of red wine from a bottle. I didn't see the label. I'm not sure it would have made a difference if I had. The significance of Chateau Faust would have been lost on me.

***

The Jinnee had left nothing to chance. Operating inside my head, he made me "see" the redemption scenario as if it had actually happened. The next time I woke up, still inside the dream, I would assume I was famous and that I had shared my bed with one of the most gorgeous women I had ever seen – Lucy from the courthouse. The Devil's own daughter.

***

Theo Jinnee was casually attending to his bunions with a Black & Decker strimmer when his mobile rang.

"Dad?"

He noted the hint of fear in his daughter's voice. "What is it, Lucy?"

"It isn't working."

"What? Why?" Furious Theo accidentally hacked off the little toe of his left foot, and sighed as a new hairy replacement bubbled up to replace it.

"Well, it started okay," she replied. "He was very pleased to see me – he remembered me from the courthouse. But he kept asking for a date. I told him we were engaged and he seemed to buy it but you'd got him very drunk and after a couple of kisses he passed out."

"Lightweight! Okay no drama. Wake him up gently, give him Alka Seltzer for his hangover laced with crystal meth – that'll kill off any disbelief and cure any saintly inhibitions – tell him how wonderfully he consummated your marriage last night and let him know you want more. Give him the ride of his life and I'll be over to sign the contract at noon. You know how important this is. If Scrimshaw's arse is yours, his soul his mine – which means the dreams stop, he won't fight Fenrir and he can't save the planet. In other words, if he fucks, God's fucked! It's a no-brainer. How could he resist his beautiful new wife? You'd give a waxwork dummy a hard-on."

"But what of something goes wrong and he doesn't buy it?"

"He has only two ways out of your bedroom, Lucy. Either he goes out corrupted or he goes out as the kind of corpse that'd make the CSI guys throw up with bits of him still splattered on the ceiling. Either way we win. You have still got the suicide vest?"

"Of course."

"Use it only as the last resort. The papers will have a field day. Terrorist Tommy killed by his own bomb, kidnapped heiress has miracle escape etc. Got it?"

"Got it."

"Good."

She put the phone down and took the explosive device out of the bathroom cabinet.

***

The small church was full of religious icons but mercifully devoid of people. Kez looked around. It had a stone floor and a wooden ceiling, and a splendid golden altar. It was obviously Catholic. She took a pew and pondered. She had no way of finding Mark and Matty, the streets were too dangerous. Her gaze settled on the angel Gabriel, she could do with a guardian angel now. She thought back to Peter and his gift of an emergency phone nestling in her duffle bag. What had he said again? You know who to call and you know the number, or something similar. Riddles! How she hated riddles…

The only numbers she could see in the church were the hymns on the board. There were ten of them, starting with 20, then an 8. She thought for a moment. If she added a nought to the start, making it 0208 that was an inner London dialling code. Worth a try? Kez had nothing to lose. She dug out the phone and started dialling.

ᛏᛏᛏ

That morning's newspapers all had different takes on the same story. The front page of the *Daily Mail* had an unflattering photograph of Tom's mum, under the headline 'Mother Of All Evil' with the subhead: Scrimbo's Mum admits 'My son is not my husband's'.

The copy read: The mother of red renegade Thomas Scrimshaw last night admitted that his real father was not the man who had raised him as her own.

The *Sun* went with 'Scrimbo Mum Shame' while the *Daily Star* screamed: 'Scrimbo Lies Nailed!' adding the revelation: 'Chippie Dad demands DNA test…'

Jeremy Kyle was apparently on stand-by.

***

Lucy had been in the bathroom quite a while, but to be honest I was glad of the peace and quiet. I was still trying to get my head around this. It seemed too good to be true. I scanned her apartment for clues but there were none. None of the pictures on the walls gave anything away either. There was one of a tropical beach, a Dali I didn't recognise (I later discovered it was called A Logician Devil), an illustration of Bob Dylan and Mick Jagger in a diner which I recognised as one of Guy Peellaert's rock dreams…but nothing to reveal anything about the girl.

I was back in bed when Lucy returned, naked except for her glossy black lace stockings and a sparkling vajazzle. My reaction was predictably immediate. "Playing tents are we darling?" she asked, her hand fondling me gently through the sheets.

She leant over and kissed me tenderly on the cheek. "I want you, husband, I want you right now…"

"And I want you Lucy, the trouble is I can't remember us getting married."

She rolled her eyes and picked up her iPhone from the top of her bedside cabinet, calling up her pictures to show the two of us as bride and groom. "There you are," she said. "That was us yesterday."

"So why can't I remember it?"

"How do I know?" she replied, a note of exasperation in her voice. "You're hung over. You had a skinful. As long as little Tommy is working I don't care and nor should you."

I scrolled through her photos. There were a few shots of us but no-one else.

"Where are all the wedding guests? Where are our families? Where's the vicar? Why are we alone?"

"Uh, because I only have eyes for you? Come on honey! You're starting to piss me off. We're married and I want you. NOW!" She dropped her voice to a whisper, and smiled: "You were so good last night, you were the best. We can do this anyway you like, me on top, you on top, doggy style, spoons, reverse cowgirl, anal…I don't mind, whatever pleases you sweetie. As my old Dad always says 'one up bum, no harm done'."

"No," I said. "This isn't right. I want it to be right, but until my memory comes back or we can prove we're married I can't do anything."

"You fucking wanker!" she exploded. "You absolutely copper-bottomed cu…That's it! You had your chance, gay-boy. We're through!"

"Lucy!"

"No. Forget it and regret it." She stormed into the bathroom and slammed the door shut.

Picture This

At that precise moment the phone by the bed rang.

"Hello...

"Tom? Is that you?"

"Keziah? How did you..."

"Never mind, I'm in trouble and I need you."

"Where are you?"

"I'm not sure, a church somewhere off Queens Road, Peckham, I think."

A wild thought crossed my mind. "Are there any pictures near you?"

"I'm right by the Madonna and child, why?"

"Stare into it."

"What?"

"Look hard at the picture and think of me."

"This is nuts!"

"What have you got to lose? Try it, concentrate and picture me."

Kez shrugged. Nothing ventured...

I thought hard about her, imagining her here with me, the warmth of her smile, the sparkle in her eyes. I had no idea if this would work but instinctively I knew it was worth a try. My head began to tingle, my veins began to bulge. I felt dizzy. I was pretty much on the verge of passing out, when Keziah materialised out of the phone.

"How the flamin'..."

I jumped out of bed and hugged her, immediately aware that I only had nothing on. Quite a lot of me went red.

"Thomas!" she said half in shock and half in amusement.

"Thomas!" said Lucy as peered in from the bathroom. "You cheating bastard!" she added, slamming the door.

"We're in trouble," said Kez.

"I know."

She tried the front door. It was deadlocked. "What can we do?"

"Hold my hand."

I had three pictures to choose from so why I swerved the paradise beach I don't know. But the two of us were sucked into the Peellaert illustration at the precise moment that Lucy came back in sporting an unbecoming stockings and suicide vest combo, making her a literal sex bomb.

By the time her suspect device exploded, we were gone.

***

The police surveillance team were shocked. The signal had just vanished. "We've lost 'Seagull'," Lobon told Arnott grimly.

"How?"

"We don't know for sure but our best guess is she must have found the bug and destroyed it."

Arnott thought for a moment and said simply "Send Harry back in."

***

Matty had managed to elude the Hell's Angels but had lost Mark and Keziah along the way. He wasn't too worried. His friends would know they'd have to regroup and would almost certainly be heading back to Bermondsey. The question was should he go ahead on foot or hang around and wait around for a 53 bus? The question was answered by someone else.

A battered red jalopy with the words 'Love' and 'Peace' painted on the sides along with a sixties-style smorgasbord of hearts and flowers pulled up alongside him. Its door was opened. "Need a lift my friend?" asked Theo Jinnee.

"Who are you?"

"I'm Theo Jinnee, a friend of Tom's. I've been helping him on his odyssey." Big smile. "He's asked me to watch out for you, Matty isn't it?"

"Where are the others?"

"Mark's on his way back to the hide-out."

"And Keziah?"

"She's fine. She's with another friend of ours."

"Thanks mate."

Matt slipped in to the passenger seat. He wasn't hurt but his body ached from the exertions of battle. Theo passed him an ice cold can of Stella Artois.

"Ta. I need this, I'm cattled. "

"I'll take you back to the safe house."

"Is Kez there?"

"Not yet." Theo's eyes twinkled. "You like her, don't you?"

"Yeah, but not like that! She's a mate. And besides she's only got eyes for Thomas, not that he knows it." He sipped the beer. "Tell you the truth it's her old woman I fancy."

"Her mother?"

"God yes. She is double gorgeous. 30something, smart, cute, a bit posh. She looks a lot like Fan Bingbing..."

"Ha, I don't know who you mean but what a great name. She sounds like a Carry On film character. And I guess you'd like to bang-bang her Fan."

He poked Matt gently in the ribs.

"Not half!"

"So why haven't you?"

"Are you serious? Man, I'm just a kid to her. I mean, I've got a lot of bunny, more front than Woolworth's my Nan used to say, but I'm out of my league with that one."

"I can help."

"What? How?"

Theo stroked his chin thoughtfully. "Mild hypnotism," he said.

"Seriously?"

"It's one of my skills." He pulled over abruptly, stopping in a bus lane. "I can do it right now if you want. All you need to say are the words 'I submit to you'."

"Ha. Leave it out, mate. Are you having a laugh?"

"Absolutely not. I am a fully qualified mentalist and it's an ethical requirement that you must say those words before I put you under."

"So I say I submit to you and you 'fluence me into a super-stud?"

"Something like that."

"Okay, I submit to you."

Theo Jinnee looked deep into Matt's eyes and clicked his fingers. Matt fell instantly into a very deep, mystical hypnotic trance.

"Right when I snap my fingers again you will wake up and have no recollection of anything I am about to say. Do you understand?"

Matt grunted.

"Okay, listen well. Matthew Cluer, if you should ever see Thomas Scrimshaw comatose or otherwise incapacitated it is your DUTY to END his life. Get that? He will be in an endangered state, and one which he cannot survive. If you do not kill him there and then Thomas will be in SEVERE pain for many weeks. Not only is it your DUTY it will also be a compassionate act of KINDNESS for a dear FRIEND. It's absolutely IMPERATIVE that you do this. It's what TOM wants you to do it. You NEED to do it to SAVE THE WORLD and the lives of everyone you ever loved. This is your destiny, Matthew, say it!"

"It's my destiny."

"Your role in life."

"My role in life."

"Say 'I'll do it'."

"I'll do it."

"Oh and yada yada when you are next alone with Keziah Smith's mother you will have the brass balls to charm her out of her yem and bang the Oriental tush off it. At that point and only at that point will you remember me and thank me unaware that the price you pay will be your immortal soul. Here endeth the session."

The driver of a 53 bus behind him tooted his horn impatiently. Theo gave him the bird and, with a further wave of his hand, a flat tyre, and drove on, smiling.

***

By coincidence Mark had been a passenger on the bus and was now forced to disembark. He was just considering whether to walk the rest of the way when a different car pulled up alongside him, only this time the driver was good old Harry, Matt's uncles' mate.

Book Three: Roads to Freedom

Rock World

We found ourselves in a rock-themed American diner, its walls adorned with guitars and platinum discs. The bar was heaving with thirsty punters decked out in denim and leathers; the juke-box in the corner blasting out their favourite songs.

"Where are we?"

"It looks like a diner."

"Nice one, Einstein. I mean where in the world are we?"

"That I couldn't tell you."

"But you brought me here!"

I shrugged. "Yeah, but I don't know how…"

"You do know you're naked though, right?"

I moved swiftly to cover my embarrassment. "You know it's cold in here, right?" I said, blushing.

No-one seemed to care, or even notice. In a corner of the heaving bar, heavily inked men in sleeveless leather jackets were playing pool for a large wad of £20 and £50 notes.

"Why it isn't a young Arnold Schwarzenegger materialising from the future," laughed a waitress.

"Who have you come to terminate, boy?"

"I erh…"

"Don't you know we have a strict dress code in this bar?"

She was wearing a leather skirt, thigh-high boots and an AC/DC t-shirt, but I choked back a smart remark and just said "Sorry"

"No drama. Stay there, stand behind your girlfriend so you don't scare the…" she looked at my groin, which I'd covered with both hands, and added "Seahorses" with a smile. "I'll get you fixed."

She returned moments later with an Iron Maiden t-shirt and a pair of black shorts. "I can't get you shoes and you'll have to go commando but at least you'll cover your modesty. You can pay for these when you settle the bill."

I looked blank.

"Well, you are eating, aren't you?"

"I'm half-starved," said Kez.

The waitress, whose badge said her name was Angelina, smiled and gestured us to a table by a window, producing two menus with a flourish. She had an incredible rose tattoo all over her left arm, so detailed you wouldn't be surprised if her tattooist's surname turned out to be da Vinci.

"Might as well eat," said Kez.

"I guess..."

"Have you seen the meals on here? There's a desert called Cakes & Sodomy!"

"That's a Marilyn Manson song."

"Everything on the menu is a song. Big Cheese, Green Onions, Honey Pie, American Pie, Curry Bun, Eggs Over Easy...oh look, Meatloaf...Ike & Tina Tuna...Johnny Marr-mite, that's a rotten pun!"

"So it's rock themed, so what?"

Angelina placed a basket of bread on the table. "I'll be right back for your order," she smiled.

"Thanks."

"It isn't just the menu though," Keziah said, lowering her voice. She pointed out the window. "We're on 53rd and 3rd...and look over there, that street is called Blackberry Way."

"Maybe it's a themed district."

"Wouldn't we have heard of it?" She glanced over the road. "There looks like a 'You Are Here' map on that corner. Come on, let's get a bigger picture."

"But I'm hungry!"

"Take some bread, we'll be back."

"What about shoes? I can't go exploring bare-footed."

Keziah thought for a moment and slipped away, returning a couple of minutes later with a pair of well-used black DM boots.

"That nice guy at the bar said you could borrow them for five minutes."

I looked over at a beer-bellied brute sitting on the stall and gave him the thumbs up. Even at a distance I couldn't help noticing that he had 'Cut here' tattooed across his neck.

"His name's Killer."

"Lovely." I gulped. "One of the Knightsbridge Killers do you suppose?" I gave Killer another smile as I slipped into the presumably battle-scarred steel-caps. Then I grabbed a roll and sprinkled some salt on it.

"We'll be back in a bit," I told Angelina.

"Yep, I spect you will. Exterminating homicidal cyborgs from the future is hungry work."

***

The electronic display map was not what we expected. By panning out we saw that we were in Angel City, whose districts apparently included Echo Beach, Rockaway Beach, Ghost Town and a town called Malice. If you chose to take the northbound Highway 61 out of the city you'd pass Holy Mountains, Kashmir and the High Falls.

We exchanged confused glances.

Over the road from us was a run-down joint called Memory Motel right next to a pub pleasantly called Murder Bar. Keziah turned back to the electronic screen and panned in.

"There's a place a few blocks down called Stairway To Heaven," she said. "To get there we have to go left down Devil Gate Drive and then over a dual carriageway called...Highway To Hell."

I gulped and chewed on my roll. My tongue felt suddenly numb.

"I don't think that was salt on the table," I said. "I think it was cocaine."

"Wishful thinking, it's probably just Peri Peri."

"Or Perry Perry, in honour of Katy?"

Keziah groaned. To the east the sky's colour was changing, golden shreds of marmalade were clearly visible – just like my dream except that right now I was absolutely sure that I was fully conscious

"We have to go that way," I said.

"Why…"

"That sky, it's in my dream."

"So that means…"

"The Oz-Troll might be there."

"And the wolf?"

"Yes," I said grimly. "And Fenrir."

We walked in silence towards the double carriageway.

"Tommy?"

"Yeah?"

"There's something I need to say to you."

I turned to face and there was a tear in her eye.

"Hey…"

"I just want you to know, before all this starts, that you mean the world to me. Tom, I think I lo…"

She was silenced by the blood-freezing sound of thunder getting louder, getting closer…No, not thunder, but something thunderous. Something mechanical.

"What the hell?"

"You really are from out of town aren't you?" It was Angelina the waitress from the rock café.

The rumbling was now deafening.

"Keep away from the road," she yelled. At that moment a giant silver ball, the size of a small house, thundered down the double carriageway at around 90mph.

"Way to go Lemmy!" she yelled.

"Praise Lemmy!" shouted a man behind me. "Go Lemster!" screamed another.

"I don't understand."

"Okay, well, you know our world is suspended in space as part of a giant natural pinball machine?"

Keziah shot me a frantic look as if to say play along with it.

"Uh huh," I said uncertainly.

"Well who do you think fires the nightly pinball?" she said, as if addressing a small stupid child. "The great god…"

"Lemmy?" Kez and I asked as one.

"Of course! Lemmy Kilmister, long may he prosper. One of the many living gods of Rock World."

"And you came after us just to tell us that?" I asked.

"No. I came after you to get Killer's boots back before he brains someone."

***

Day 27 Harry and Mark sat up in the safe house kitchen sipping malt whisky, waiting for the others to turn up.

"So you couldn't get into New Cross?" Harry asked casually as he sparked up a spliff.

"Not a chance, there were way too many of them for the three of us to take on. I mean, we tried but it was like…that film the 300 in reverse. It was us trying to smash past hundreds of the bastards."

Harry nodded. "Who were they? And why did they want to stop you?"

"No idea who they were but they clearly wanted to keep us away from Tom."

"Why do you think he's there?"

Mark paused. "It's hard to say this without sounding daft," he said finally. "But we think he's communicating with us through our dreams."

"Eh? You're having a laugh, Marky!"

"I know, weird, right? But he was seeing all sorts of bizarre things in his dreams before, and the messages we've deciphered point strongly to one street in New Cross."

"Which is?"

"Lupino Lane."

The secret policeman grinned and topped up Mark's glass.

"We think we know the number too, so…"

There was a rat-tat-tat on the front door.

"I'll get it," said Harry. He approached the door gingerly, picking up a baseball bat along the way.

It was Matty, who looked exhausted. The three hugged.

"Thank god you're here," said Matt. "No idea how I got back. I've just woken up on a park bench. I'm cream-crackered! I must have walked it."

"Any sign of Kez, Matt?" asked Mark anxiously.

"I was going to ask you the same thing. No, nothing."

"She'll come back here, won't she?"

"Where else could she go?"

"So Matt, Mark here says you need to get to an address in New Cross."

"We do, mate."

"So I'm wondering why you're trying to do it on foot at night, where you've got to pass all those lowlife firms, when it would be far easier to get there…"

"By train!" Mark said. "In daylight…"

"Exactly."

"And Lupino Lane is just a few hundred yards from the station," Matt chimed in. "So tomorrow, that's what we do."

"Wait," said Mark. "What if we get the same train that Tom used to get? I don't know why, but it feels like we'd have more chance of getting there that way."

"Well, there would be loads of commuters, so it'd be easy to get lost in the crowd," Matt said slowly.

"And you wouldn't have the gangs of wannabe yobbos hanging around then," added Harry.

"Right," said Mark. "That settles it. We'll get the 5.16 from Waterloo East."

"Unless it's cancelled," grinned Matty. "From memory it often was."

"And I'll come with you, for back-up," said Harry. "It's what yer uncles would want, Matt."

"That's really good of you mate."

"You're more than welcome. Gold watch?"

"Cheers!"

***

"We should have asked her the way," Keziah complained.

"What exactly would we have said, Kez? Excuse me missus, we're a bit lost could you direct us back to the planet earth in the year 2014? Or is it 2015 now?"

In the distance, the marmalade sky was slowing obscured by a spreading purple haze.

"That's where we have to go," I said. "C'mon Kez. This is where the dream ends."

"Will we be safe?"

"Of course," I lied. "Look there's New Cross station."

The platform sign was visible through the mist. But I knew safety wouldn't come into this equation. I heard a wolf howl, and felt a shiver of fear. Out of the corner of my eye, under the New Cross sign, I spotted the twisted, leering face of the Oz-Troll.

"On second thoughts, you hang back here, Kez. I'll be okay."

"But..."

"Don't worry! I know what's coming next." Oh yeah, I did all right. Next comes the part where I clobber the troll and take on the wolf...

***

In New Cross, Theo Jinnee was busy studying his ornate three-dimensional chess board; thinking, planning, working out a strategy. He was a dozen mental manoeuvres ahead before he felt satisfied. Only then, finally, did he make one move on each of the levels and allow himself a smile. Theo felt like a matador toying sadistically with a badly wounded, particularly stupid bull.

Channelling Yeats, he said wistfully "The blood-dimmed tide is loosed and everywhere/The ceremony of innocence is drowned." Then he cackled like a pantomime villain.

***

I was girding my loins for the battle to come when an absurdly large hand came from behind and swept me right off my feet.

The mega-mitt belonged to Iron Maiden's metal monster Eddie somehow made flesh. But before he could do anything

158

more, he was booted out of the way by an even larger Ozzy Osbourne.

With an ear-splitting belch, Ozzy grabbed me and guffawed. "It's too soon," he said as he tightened his grip on my ankles and swung me around repeatedly like a rag doll.

I was on the verge of passing out when he let go, propelling me up, up and away towards outer space.

Up I shot through the stratosphere and then the thermosphere praying to whatever God might listen to somehow make me safe.

Why wasn't the cold killing me, by the way? Was this proof that the Almighty was doing his bit for me? Maybe it would help if I'd believed in Him in the first place...Maybe I should try praying to Zeus instead. Or was that like a hypochondriac asking for a placebo?

***

Back on Rock World, the Oz-Troll moved towards Keziah playing with its huge gnarled wart-encrusted member. "Come to papa, sweet lips," the vile creature chuckled, its nostrils inflating and deflating like a manic accordion, its puny brain clouded by penile dementia. "Come lose that sweet virgin cherry. Once you've had troll your life's never dull..."

His laugh was horrible, like a sewer bubbling over. His breath smelt similar but not quite as pleasant.

The troll's turgid todger stuck out as rigid as a poker but many times thicker. Kez turned to run but lost her footing. As she fell, her hand struck something hard in the pockets of her Levis. She still had the phone! In desperation Keziah pulled it out and hit 9-9-9.

With a blast of Massive Attack's Unfinished Symphony, a bright celestial door appeared in a flash to her left and Peter, her amiable benefactor, shimmered into view just as the Oz-Troll was spitting into his warty hands for lubrication. Moving with a grace that belied his size, Peter hoisted Kez off the floor as effortlessly as a circus strongman lifting a newborn pup and transported her through the portal, back into a long peaceful sweet-smelling corridor inside 22 Lupino Lane.

"There, there," he said, his strong arms comforting her. "You're quite safe now, me duck."

Keziah sobbed ill-defined words of gratitude, and then noticed that Tommy's comatose body was lying dormant in the corridor ahead of them.

"Tom? Is he okay? Wait, that monster threw him up, so how did he get here?"

"He didn't exactly. Thomas has been here quite a while sweet child."

"Wait, if Tom is here, who was I with?"

"That was Thomas. You were with him in his dream."

"I was in his dream?"

"You often are."

"How is that even possible?"

"Don't try and work out the science of magic."

Keziah drew herself up to her full 5ft 5. "I'm sorry, Peter," she said. "You've helped me a lot and I'm very grateful for that, but please don't fob me off. Not after all that we've been through, and all that Thomas has still go to go through. Tell me the truth please."

"By all means. Thomas has been targeted by a nasty piece of inhuman malignity who you might know as Loki, Satan, or Old Harry. This black-hearted parasite is a jinnee who uses humans as a jewel wasp would use a cockroach. Do you know what I mean?"

Kez shook her head. "No, please explain."

"The jewel wasp incapacitates its victim allowing its larva to consume it from the inside. It does it with two stings. Loki who is currently posing as Thomas's protector Theo Jinnee – see all the clues are there – does it with dreams. Maybe toxoplasmosis is a better comparison, as that also subverts instincts. Either way the host body is generally powerless to resist the mind-altering venom. The cockroach is doomed. Having breached its defences, the wasp steers it back to his own burrow and lays its egg on its abdomen. Eventually it is chewed to death by the newborn wasp-larva.

"Theo/Loki's eggs are temptations, sweet-coated poisons that appeal to our baser instincts. He has hooked countless dull American evangelists with them…

"The difference between cockroaches and the likes of us is that a very small number of humans, generally one every millennium, has the moral fibre and the inner goodness to resist. It's as clear to us as it is to Loki that Thomas has that potential, my job is to help him as much as possible."

"So Tom's dreams?"

"Are Loki's doing. But like Tom's mission they are also deadly dangerous and very real. By which I mean his dream worlds all actually exist in our great multiverse as other dimensions."

Keziah looked blank.

"Rock World exists."

Thomas Sees All

I can't begin to explain how this happened, but my upward trajectory came to an abrupt end and I found myself standing on some kind of barren dusty ground that looked much like you'd imagine the surface of the moon to be. But that was impossible, of course. If I'd hit the moon at that speed I would have been splattered like a fly on a windscreen. And I definitely wouldn't be breathing. I looked up and for a moment I saw the earth, beautiful, blue, benign and bewitching in the night sky. I gasped. Then the madness began again. My vision blurred abruptly. It was as if the walls of one reality were disintegrating, throwing open a thousand other realities and more that exploded around me like one breath-taking, mind-boggling, gigantic panoramic kaleidoscope.

Several frankly terrifying minutes followed before, by focusing and breathing slowly, I was able to slow down the sensual eruption and concentrate on the different scenarios one by one.

I saw earth's near future first, a future of arable deserts, farmed sea beds and Californian independence. Then a thousand different earth futures paraded before my eyes, including scores of possible apocalypses – death by asteroid, defeat by robot take-over, doom by nuclear war, pandemics and super-volcanoes...but not by man-made climate change, that was way too far-fetched.

I saw earths under the iron heel of various dictators, their jackbooted armies locked in perpetual warfare – a permanent war economy, built on hatred, greed and lies in the service of self-appointed leaders, one of whom looked uncannily like Fuehrer Theo Jinnee.

And then I saw another future built on freedom and enterprise, with power devolved down canton-style to local areas. The bureaucratic state had all but withered away.

There were no laws telling consenting adults what they could do in their own bedrooms. And no large armed forces; instead every citizen was trained in self-defence with a small highly trained military as back-up. Self-reliance and self-improvement were this world's guiding principles. Trade boomed, start-ups abounded and freedom of speech was sacrosanct. It was a world without fear. Paradise on earth? A new Jerusalem?

The limitless vision shifted. I found myself standing unharmed in liquid methane showers on Titan, in meteorite downpours on Mars and in monstrous anticyclones on Jupiter...then I saw further, beyond the solar system, into other galaxies where other civilizations flourished, some barbarous, some benign. I was gasping for breath when I felt a hand on my shoulder.

The hand belonged to a very old, white-haired, bearded man who seemed to radiate contentment, love and sheer simple awesomeness.

"Are you...God?"

"I am We," he said. His large green eyes were as warm and twinkly as a faun's in a Disney cartoon.

"I don't understand what is happening here."

"Why would you, with your finite human brain?"

"Why am I seeing all this?"

"I am letting you see things as I see them, Thomas. Reality is far, far bigger than you could ever imagine." He smiled. "You humans see less than a billionth of the electromagnetic spectrum – what you call visible light. Everything else that is out there, and there is a lot of it, can only be seen at different frequencies. Gamma rays, radio waves, microwaves, x-rays…Wait a second, I shall turn it off."

The swirling psychedelic matrix folded in on itself and vanished and I found myself sitting in an armchair in a cosy living room next to a roaring fire. "Pot of tea?" the old man asked.

"Thank you."

"Builders' is best." Those big eyes seemed to radiate waves of Zen harmony.

"Normally all of that would be invisible to you but it doesn't mean it isn't there," he said. "Some people sense other elements and interpret them as something they're not. They see visible images as colourful auras or 'ghosts' or aliens or visions or whatever, but mostly the data streams just pass through you all completely undetected. Your heads couldn't cope. All that 'cosmic algebra' would blow your minds."

"So you see everything?"

"I do, Thomas. That's what omniscience means."

"And so you're not human?"

"Far from it. I'm not even really here. I'm a physical manifestation of the life force assuming a pleasing humanoid shape for your benefit."

"Thank you… But why? Why me?"

"Haven't you figured it out yet? Tommy, I am your father…"

***

The walls of the sitting room disintegrated sending my mind on a vast cosmic tour, way beyond alternative earths. On I looked, moved faster through the multiverse, broadening my view, searching for answers until everything clicked into place. I saw the answers to all the questions that have troubled human philosophers since the dawn of our time. Suddenly I understood what white beard had meant, I saw everything clearly. I realised that:

i) There was no God, no singular creator. What we call God is actually the soul of the universe, the cosmic animating force.

ii) That God exists timelessly to the limits of the universe and beyond.

iii) God is the universal life-force that touches us all, a divinity that exists within us and without us.

iv) Similarly there was no "after-life" as imagined by religions and spiritualists. But our essence, our spirit does not die; after physical death it returns to the cosmos to be reborn in various forms.

v) All things are linked, animals, plants, rivers, minerals, planets, the elements.

vi) All is within God and God is within all.

vii) There is a meaning to human life, evolution towards the next form.

Man will become something better, something stronger and smarter, the superman...man will keep growing...men will become demi-gods.

Unless, I realised, Theo's forces of darkness derail the process and return mankind to our baser instincts; to a state where he can divide and rule. All would be decided in the battles to come, and somehow I had become important in this. My battle was mankind's battle. My victory would clear the way for the next stage of human progress; my defeat would set the process back 1,000 years.

***

"Rock World exists?" Keziah looked dumbfounded. "So wait, are you saying that there's a universe where an entire planet is somehow built on the back of a naturally occurring pinball machine which is played, once every evening, by the giant

164

representation of Lemmy from Motörhead?" She laughed at the absurdity of the idea.

"Well yes but I believe they let Iggy Pop take a shot every now and then when Lemmy is otherwise engaged."

"No way!"

"Way!"

Peter sighed. "There are more universes than you can count, my dear; an infinite number in fact, many of them are unconstrained by the laws of Newtonian physics, with different atoms and gravitational fields and so on. Pretty much anything the human mind can image is happening or has happened somewhere."

He paused and looked at her. Keziah was still awake and still listening. He carried on. "What you see here as iron rules, the 'laws of physics', are just parochial by-laws in the grand cosmic scheme of things. There are a million worlds in as many dimensions where very different Keziahs get on with their lives and in some of them your organs are externalised. In others you are closer to a lizard…"

He watched the confusion spread across her face. "I didn't say it was going to be easy, Kez. I just said it would be the truth."

"Wow," she said. "Are you Morpheus?"

Peter smiled. "Nothing so glamorous."

"What about that troll thing with Ozzy Osbourne's face?"

"Probably just a manticore," he shrugged.

She'd Google that when she got home. If she ever did, that is.

"So hold on, what happens if Tom fails? If he loses to the wolf and the Devil?"

"Darkness," Peter signed. "Darkness, despair and desolation. But don't fret, duchess, New Cross, that's the key to it all."

Valhalla, I Am Coming

I was back at New Cross, and mercifully there was no sign of Keziah. God, I could kick myself for putting her through this.

Almost immediately the Oz-Troll was coming at me, as hairy and diseased as he had seemed in my dreams. I caught a blast of his rancid breath before the creature produced his pockmarked scrotum and began to pop out his testicles like a succession of ping-pong balls. He seemed surprised when I didn't react and shocked when I kicked his transformed dancing baby testicles straight into touch.

The troll clearly didn't know that I knew what was coming…

As he turned into Calista Flockhart, I kicked his/her legs away and, ignoring the increasingly psychedelic sky and the screaming stones beneath my feet, I moved towards the nun who had now appeared some thirty yards away. Freeje! When she laughed, the screaming stopped. She looked magnificent. Freeje's smile – or as I suspected her lookalike's smile – spurred me on.

I started to sprint but my path was blocked by her double. As expected this one metamorphosed into the Oz-Troll who I swotted away before he could get into his lame Limp Bizkit schtick.

As in the dream, as I got closer to Freeje I seemed to grow taller, broader, and stronger. I could feel my biceps expanding, rippling away under my Iron Maiden t-shirt. My shoes had become leather boots, my shirt an armoured breastplate. My trousers had gone, and instead I was wearing a warrior tunic. A splendid two-handed sword appeared at my side. I was ready; ready to ruck.

"Tiwaz," she said as I reached her. "Take me…"

It took all of my self-control to ignore her request. As she moved to kiss me, I gently but firmly pushed her to one side and carried on. The wolf's howl became louder. I was very near. And then I saw him.

***

Peter had shown Keziah a modest section of 22 Lupino Lane including the garden and its eyesore of a ladder – "I keep telling Jacob to move it" – and then he'd let her rest for a couple of hours before waking her with a cup of strong tea and her favourite chocolate brownie.

"Have you heard from Thomas?" she asked. She was anxious and slightly afraid.

"No, but it has begun," he said.

"What has?"

"The battle. The end game. Here, and there. It's all in Tom's hands now. But don't worry, he has allies. He has friends. Freeje is ready. She'll be joining him soon, and so might we be."

Keziah look puzzled.

"You knew her as the Rock Chick," Peter smiled. "We know her as the Holy Ghost."

***

Fenrir was not so much a wolf as a man-wolf. Specifically the man-wolf from my nightmares, the prosecutor in my court case, Stannard von Wolfson.

His lip curled back in a snarl and he came straight at me, grunting and spitting. I caught him with a straight left that put him off-balance, and kicked down hard on his left knee as he fell. He hit the floor screaming in pain, but rolled over and came back at me smashing me with a left right combination. His sharp nails ripped the skin across my forehead.

I don't know how I had learned to fight like this, but boy was I grateful. I felt so strong, so vital. Both of us had swords but neither of us felt inclined to use them. Yet. This was it, no weapons just fists.

We both staggered back. I had a reach advantage and fired off a couple of decent rights. His head was too large for his body. It made a good target. His right cheek had started to look like a chopped hamburger but he kept coming at me, opening his big gummy gob as if he were trying to paralyse me with his fetid breath or distract with his mouth full of sharp, irregular teeth.

I pulled my left arm back and flung a fierce left hook. It missed him but I stepped closer and hooked again, connecting with his hairy jaw. I kept swinging at that big head, backing him into a corner. I threw a left, a right and an overhand right. I had him, I knew it!

Then he got past my defences and smashed me with a right so hard that it hit my jaw and went all the way down to my toes.

I went down like a sack of spuds.

"Who are ya? Who are ya?" Wolfson sneered, triumphantly. "I thought you were going to be hard to beat, but you're nothing, boy, you're the shit on my shoes."

Always a mistake to make triumphant speeches while your opponent is still conscious, I feel. As he ranted on I kicked his feet away from him and he went down, hitting that big fat head of his against a rock.

I got back to my feet. My face was a mask of blood from the cut above my left eye. It felt like we'd fought ten rounds in one.

My right eye was swollen, I was aware that blood was trickling from my nose and mouth and my kidneys hurt. But the wolf-man was down. I raised my sword to smite him and was knocked sideways, by the Oz-Troll. The beast slammed me to the ground and started to batter me. My sword clattered to a stop a couple of yards away. His blows came in a flurry.

"I am going to peel off your skin, rip out your veins and hang you by them," he said. "Then I'll feed the rest of you to the dogs and leave your bones for them to piss on."

The troll howled triumphantly and began throwing more punches at me. I held my arms up in defence but I was tired and he was rested and strong. I knew time was running out for me.

Oh hell. I've let every down. I tried, god knows I tried, but I just wasn't up to the job.

The Oz-Troll beat down on me relentlessly. I didn't have the energy to fight back.

Suddenly I was aware of someone else behind him. Fenrir? Come to finish me off? No. It was Freeje. Strong, magnificent, beautiful…and using my sword to decapitate the troll.

"Here," she said, handing me the weapon. "You need this, to finish the job."

I staggered to my feet and took the sword just as a dazed Fenrir reached for his. Freeje stood back – she had to – and watched. What happened next was like the fight scene in the film Scaramouche only significantly less like an armed ballet. We cut, we thrust, and we hacked. It was vicious, deadly and exhausting. I lost track of time.

If my left eye hadn't been blinded by blood and sweat I would have seen the stroke that cut deep into my left hand. And if he hadn't been so pleased with himself he might have stopped my response, the righteous coup de grace that went straight through the wolf-man's heart and ended it all.

Freejc came straight to my side. She'd torn her skirt and started to wrap up my hand in a bid to keep the wound clean.

"I'll lose it," I said, glumly. "It's written."

"Not in this reality," she smiled. "We've got BUPA."

We both laughed. "Well done, Thomas, I knew you'd do it."

I wanted to kiss her, but didn't. "How did you get here?" I asked.

"You summoned me," she said simply.

"When?"

"In the pub, the Dark Lantern. Don't you remember? You distinctly said, 'I need some Holy Ghost please'..."

"What? Oh, yeah. Maybe. When I was ordering breakfast. Holy Ghost, toast."

"Well there you are then. Lucky you did because if you hadn't I wouldn't have been able to spring you from those oafs at the court house, or follow you here."

"Well, I never," I coughed. I felt so weak.

"But what am I doing chatting away? You can't stay here. You have to be somewhere else. Or rather you have to be 'here' somewhere else and you have to be there now."

The nun started to run her hands through the air over my body but I passed out before I could work out why.

**

The story made Sky News' 5pm headlines. Presenter Faye Curley said solemnly: "Thomas Scrimshaw, the fugitive anarchist known as Scrimbo, has been found at a railway siding at New Cross station in South East London. His comatose body was spotted shortly after 2pm but police have been unable to reach him. Scrimshaw has not moved at all since he was sighted. Over now to our man on the scene Darren McCartney, Darren…"

"Thanks Faye, yes it certainly looks like Scrimshaw and he does appear to be breathing, albeit weakly. But he is absolutely caked with blood. He has obviously been involved in some kind of hellish violence. Unfortunately the police can't apprehend him because he seems to be surrounded by some electronic force field."

"A force field?"

"Yes. There are police scientists at the scene attempting to turn it off."

"Is Scrimbo alone, Darren?"

"I can't see anyone else inside the force field, however his presence here is causing quite a commotion as members of the public, including a large mob of drunken hooligans and punks hostile to the police are gathering around the scene. Police have drafted in more officers to hold them at bay."

***

One avid Sky News viewer not delighted by the headline report was local detective Theo Jinnee, who moved swiftly to mobilise his own forces to claim and destroy Thomas Scrimshaw's body. It was vital that the boy was not revived.

Crazy Train

Harry's phone bleeped the moment that they emerged at Waterloo station from the bowels of the underground. He read the message and looked grim. "It's Thomas," he said. "He's turned up at New Cross station but he's hurt."

"We need to get there."

"We've got six minutes before the train leaves platform 1 at Waterloo East," said Mark.

"Well come on!"

They pelted across the concourse, up the escalator and across the bridge, reaching the platform just as the 5.16 was pulling in. There were no seats. Mark noticed the other commuters: a couple of secretaries, a guy with an MP3 player that was way too loud, a sneezing building worker, a thin-faced middle-aged bore, a large woman who was five foot high and six foot wide. And orange...she looked like one of the Wotsits she was eating.

"This is Tom's carriage," he said softly as the train departed. "I recognise these people from the way he used to talk about them."

"And I recognise these two," said Harry, indicating two tough-looking men who were making their way down the carriage towards them. "Gents, I'd like you to meet Bone, who is Millwall, ex-Regiment and very nearly house-trained, and this is Gonzo, so-called for reasons I hope you'll experience first-hand when all this is behind us."

They shook hands warmly.

"I thought we might need some back-up," Harry smiled. "How's it looking chaps?"

"We've checked the whole train," said Bone. "No hostiles."

"Gentleman, we should reach our destination at 5.25pm. Nine minutes."

The train pulled up with a jerk.

"London Bridge," said Gonzo. "It's not supposed to stop here."

"Could just be the disruption up ahead..."

Three minutes passed before train started to move again. "Look who it is," Mark said to Matty as Joey Bishop and a grizzled sidekick came lurching down the carriage. He was carrying a hunting knife.

"I've got this," said Bone. Moving fast, he grabbed Bishop's hand and dug his nails in deep. Joey yelped like a dog and dropped the blade. The handle was wet, glistening with his sweat. He was nervous then.

"Who sent you?" asked Harry.

"Go fuck yourself." Bishop spat in Harry's face. His troglodyte sidekick threw a right hook at Bone who clumped him around the ear hard, perforating his ear drum. The thug staggered forward, off balance and Harry knocked him spark out. The two secretaries were screaming.

Joey Bishop stepped back and blew a whistle. "It's show time," he leered.

Members of his gang started coming from both directions. But the train was too crowded for their numbers to count. For the next six minutes the fighting five picked them off one by one.

"That was like the Southeastern version of the 300," laughed Matty, as the train shuddered to a halt. "Mark didn't even have to do his weird body-hopping thang." He grinned broadly. "Is that all they've got?"

"I don't think so," said Harry. "Let's move to the front of the train."

***

They were held up again just outside New Cross station. After five minutes Matty suggested they disembark and walk the rest of the way. But as he tried to figure out how to open the doors in an emergency, the train lurched off, lifting right off the track.

Commuters on platform C watched open-mouthed in horror as the train climbed sluggishly up into the sky, jerking along like some monstrous mechanical marionette until it vanished abruptly mid-air.

"How?" gasped Mark.

"No idea," Matt replied.

Along it went, through a dark tunnel before emerging and heading downwards at stomach-dropping speed, through a booming waterfall and past menacing rock formations.

"Look out!" Harry shouted as a huge boulder rolled down a dusty hill towards them on a certain collision course. They braced themselves for an impact that never came.

"It's like we're on a rollercoaster," he said.

"Like that Disney one," agreed Mark. "Is it called Thunder Mountain or something?" He couldn't think, he was still trying to take in how a London to Kent commuter train had reached a dilapidated Old West mining town and, if that wasn't weird enough, had also somehow simultaneously morphed into an amusement park ride.

He and Matt were strapped into one seat, Harry and Bone were in the car in front, Gonzo brought up the rear, with Joey Bishop and his gang several seats back and the fat lady from the real train wetting herself behind them. The screams of the two secretaries were drowned out by the loud refrain of a song Mark recognised as ZZ Top's Tube Snake Boogie that was blasting out of strategically placed speakers.

As the ride slowed, he studied the scenery they were rolling past. The creatures on the mountainside – howling coyotes, tail-rattling snakes, dangling possums and a goat chewing a stick of dynamite – were clearly animatronics. There was a large wooden sign ahead. 'Danger! Keep Out! Blast Area!' it said, but the train kept chugging on regardless; on and on through a mixture of sound lighting and fog effects into a massive exploding fireball at the end of a collapsing tunnel that never quite fell in. They felt the heat but there was no pain to follow.

Mark caught his breath. "Look," he said. "That sign says…"

"Dusty Hill's Mountain of Thrills."

"No, not that one, that big one over there says Rock World…."

"Are those giant statues of ZZ Top?"

"I don't think they're statues, they're waving at us…"

"This is crazy!"

"Hang on, we're going down!" The train didn't so much descend as plummet.

Hammer Of The Gods

Twas Doomsday and Lucifer's hordes
Did revel through the night
The second coming would not come

Their enemy was too slight

Keziah had materialised inside the force field at the precise moment that the 5.16 from Waterloo East had juddered to an unexpected stop outside of New Cross station. In amazement, she watched the train re-start and start to take off like a slow moving jet before disappearing before her eyes. She might have wondered about it a bit more if she hadn't then seen the trolls. Not one or two or even scores of them but hundreds of the ugly beasts; a vast army of simple-minded brutes with one mission – the obliteration of Thomas Scrimshaw.

The watching public who had gathered around the force field started to panic and scatter as the fearsome troll massive materialised. The Met police followed suit, leaving just two plucky TV news cameramen between them and their comatose target. They didn't stay long either. The lead troll snapped off a length of railway track as casually as you might bend plasticine and had started to use it as a battering ram in a bid to smash their way through the force field. Keziah gripped Thomas's hand and prayed her luck would hold.

It was at that moment that a train from a fairground rollercoaster crash-landed right in front of her, ploughing into the first lines of the troll assault force. Matty and Mark were right near the front of it. Yes!

"Come on!" shouted Matty as he leapt from the wreckage and ran straight at the trolls, taking out ten more of the creatures. Behind him, Mark stared straight at the troll with the length of track, took over his simple mind, and began to use the weapon on the others; while Harry and two other heavy-looking guys began slugging it out with them one on one.

At that moment a sound system in a near-by squat started to pump out brain-bludgeoning non-stop techno, as if to supply the fight with its own soundtrack, the vicious bass lines driving on the brutal action. The battling band of brothers seemed to inspire the cops who charged back into the fray with batons and tasers. Other train passengers followed suit, including a large-bellied building worker. Even a few of the punks got stuck in. It wasn't so much a rainbow alliance, thought Kez, as a Rambo one.

***

It wasn't all good news. The force field had been partially breached. There was a gap in the side about five feet up, wide enough for a man to climb through if not yet a troll. Inside Thomas's body had begun to twitch and convulse, Keziah gripped his hand tighter. She knew that even her ability to channel fortune couldn't hold back a thousand-strong pack of marauding trolls.

The tide of battle seemed to turn in humanity's favour, but not for long. In rapid succession the troll with the railway track was smacked to the ground and overwhelmed by his fellows. Then Kez watched Matty get smothered by about twenty of the brutes. Meanwhile Harry, the two other men and the police were being forced back by the sheer weight of numbers.

The heavens darkened as the fighting continued, with black clouds blocking out the last of the evening sun, surely a portent of impending doom.

"Thomas," she said. "You have to come back. We need you, the world needs you, we love you." She hesitated and added softly "I love you" just as Peter materialised behind her.

"How goes it?" he asked.

"Badly," she replied. "Look…"

"Oh I don't know…"

Joey Bishop and his gang had come storming off the crashed train and had started attacking the trolls with knives, coshes and ammonia – the tools of their trade. They weren't alone. From the main road other mobs joined the fray, skinheads, casuals, punks, the Peckham Boys…

"The Gangs of New Cross," Peter smiled.

"But they hate us," said Keziah.

"They might well, but this is their patch, their turf. They won't surrender it to Loki's troll battalions."

"How did Mark and Matty get here? They dropped right out of the sky!"

"The black magic that let in the trolls shifted inter-dimensional tectonic plates. Your friends' train was re-routed, rather delightfully I suspect. You'll see it's reverted to its earthly form now."

"So where are the army?" she said as she watched a troll take out a flick-knife wielding geriatric Teddy Boy. "Where are the Paras, the SAS?"

"This whole area is now contained within a kind of giant bubble, courtesy Loki. No-one else can reach us now. The forces your friends have brought along or attracted are all we have."

Keziah's face drained of colour and she tightened her grip on Thomas's hand. The fighting was fierce and hand-to-hand. The only reinforcements were stragglers from the train, including a skull-headed man she recognised as Dugash from Tom's work. Once again she saw things improve only to have the hope dashed out of her heart.

"There are just too many of them," she said.

Peter said nothing; he was looking up at the thunder clouds and praying.

***

In an entirely different dimension, across a burning rainbow bridge, others were watching the earthly carnage.

"This is wrong," a man with a golden mane of hair said to his father. "This is Loki's doing."

"Then it must be undone," Odin replied.

"So mote it be."

I Am The Resurrection

"Wake up Thomas, please," Keziah said for maybe the thirtieth time. "Wake up, I love you."

Nothing. He was still out cold.

If this were the Lord Of The Rings, she thought, I'd be able to blow on a butterfly and summon giant eagles to rescue us. I haven't even got a house fly to work with.

Ahead of her Kez saw a troll take out the Peckham gang leader with the caterpillar eyebrows with one fatal blow.

As the youth fell the eyebrows turned into butterflies and flew away.

Another troll had found the hole in the force field and was smashing it wider with its fat, bleeding fists. They were jinxed, bedevilled, undone.

***

Matty saw his chance and took it, battering the troll out of the way, and clambering through the hole.

"Matt!" Kez squealed with delight. "Thank god! Tom is alive! We have to keep him safe."

Matty looked at Thomas and his eyes glazed over. "It's time," he said softly. He pulled a face like a mask of death.

"Matty? What's going on?"

"I have to kill Thomas."

"Why?"

"For his own good."

"What?"

"It's my destiny."

"No!"

She blocked Matt's route, but he rushed straight at her head down.

Peter pulled her from harm's way. "It isn't your Matt," he said. "He's been got at, look at his eyes, he's enchanted."

Matt turned away and stood legs akimbo as he began building himself up for a final death charge. Desperate, Keziah ran in front of him and kicked him hard in his most tender area. She didn't take the Bull by the horn, she joked later, but she did take him out by the balls.

Matt doubled up and fell. He didn't get up, he was out cold. Kez grinned. "Surely it's an elementary evolutionary cock-up for you boys to carry your precious genetic treasure chest in a small, delicate parcel of unprotected flesh dangling outside the protection of your bodies…" she said.

"Not sure why you passed out though," she went on. "Was it the pain, Peter, or something to do with the spell he was under?"

There was no reply. When she turned around, Peter had gone. She was alone again with Thomas. So all she had done was buy them some time; that trick would only work once. She tried to wield Tom's sword but she couldn't even lift it. When Matt came to, they were done for.

Keziah felt a tear well up in her right eye and didn't stop it from splashing on to Thomas's face.

***

My eyes blinked open. "Where am I?" I said.

"Tom!" Keziah hugged me tightly and planted a smacker on my lips just as a bolt of lightning struck twenty feet ahead of us. Where once had been a large oak tree now stood a giant, burning hammer.

I surveyed the scene, taking in the mayhem and carnage. Trolls! A whole army of them! The fighting was savage, the odds weren't great.

Another huge bolt of lightning followed, taking out a hundred head of the terrifying tide. Then another, then another… The troll dead formed a barricade around the force field. Nothing would penetrate that tonight.

Inspired by the enemy's mounting casualties the human forces, now bolstered by Millwall Bushwhackers, Hell's Angels and the Met police riot squad, all of whom had made it to the battle on foot after being caught up in the traffic jam caused by Beelzebub's bubble, redoubled their efforts and forced the remnants of the now panicking assault force back through the satanic wormhole that had spawned them.

"Thomas," said a disembodied voice so deep and strong it seemed to shake the ground. "Odin owns them all! Victory is ours. Victory is yours."

***

As she helped Thomas to his feet Kez couldn't help noticing how different he felt. How muscular, strong and powerful. How...

"Hard luck Tommee!"

I knew that voice. It was a troll. No. It was the Oz-Troll.

"But you're dead," I said.

"There is more than one of We," the creature replied, fingering a lethal blade. "This is where your story ends," it cackled, adding "Hail..."

Before he could say "Satan", a giant fist materialising behind his head and knocked it back through the wormhole too. I recognised the fist from a poster on my bedroom wall. It belonged to Iron Maiden's Eddie who presumably hadn't materialised fully in our world for copyright reasons. (You wouldn't want to cross Rod Smallwood, I can tell you.)

Eddie laughed as he vanished. The laugh proved infectious.

Keziah gave me another hug just as Matt regained consciousness. Her face – so young and so beautiful, why hadn't I noticed that before? – flooded with concern. But Mathew smiled when he saw us. Whatever demonic spell he'd been under had gone. As had the force field...

I looked at Keziah. "Kez? You love me?"

She blushed. I smiled. We kissed. Matt applauded. I smiled some more.

Hands were pulling down the troll corpses, clearing the way for us. The faces of the ragged human army beamed as we emerged hand in hand. They clapped and parted before us like a jubilant pantomime cast welcoming the leading actors back to the stage for their final bows.

***

The next day's Times had the full exclusive state-approved story of how the people of South London, led and mobilised by Thomas Scrimshaw and his young friends had foiled an alien plot to invade the earth.

Rather than being 'anarchists', thundered the editorial, the Scrimbo group were 'part of a secretive organisation known as Nemesis working on behalf of Her Majesty's government and should be honoured as national heroes.' Over the next week, the Fleet Street newspapers were united in their praise for the pardons that followed, with many calling for the four 'young lions' to each receive the George Cross in recognition of their conspicuous courage in circumstances of extreme danger.

Unfortunately the full details of Operation Nemesis were covered by a DA-Notice and could not be made public for at least fifty years.

Day 35 "And that was it," smarmy morning TV host Philip Blofeld was saying. "You fell in love."

"We fell in love," I said with a smile.

"You got a full pardon for your conviction and an official apology from the Metropolitan Police. The whole nation fell in love with you too. Did that surprise you?"

"What can I say?" I grinned modestly. "It's not every day that someone saves the world from a deadly alien invasion force."

"And we thank you for that. You know you were out cold for two full days there, don't you?

"I didn't know that. I kind of lost track of time..."

"We understand that time ran at a different pace inside the bubble," Keziah explained. "It can do that, apparently."

Blofeld smiled at her condescendingly and looked back at me.

"And on the third day you rose again."

"I still had work to do," I said, deliberately ignoring the reference to Corinthians.

"So what are your plans now?" he asked.

"To help people," I said. "To do good stuff."

"A little bird tells me the two of you are getting married," Blofeld's bosomy co-host Holly Willenbody twittered.

"Next month," Keziah replied.

"Congratulations! And the others?"

"Mark and Matty will be there. We'll have two best men. Freeje is my maid of honour. Our friend Peter will officiate at the ceremony."

"Where are you going for your honeymoon?" Philip asked.

"Oh, a holiday resort," I said. "A little place we love called Rock World."

After the broadcast, while Kez was having her make-up removed, Blofeld took me to one side in the corridor and grabbed my arm hard.

"I will get you," he said, his dead eyes flashing with menace. For a split second, before he walked away, his face turned into the face of Theo Jinnoo. But he hasn't yet.

Some Might Say: An Epilogue

In a small theatre, in god alone knows where, two strange humanoid comedians cheered as the final frame of the film ending.

"Woo! He saved the planet!" hollered Lenoman. "He beat the Trolls, he got the girl! What's not to like?"

"What's not to like is you, bub," snapped Letterman. "Ya big birdbrain. You spoilt the whole goddamn screening whooping like a jackass and chomping on pop corn and hot dogs."

"I'm having fun!"

"Wowee, your lack of life just flashed before my eyes!"

"Hey, do you think these guys want to know what happened next?" He pointed straight up at you.

"Nah, we might get another book out of this."

"What if I just give them a little taste?"

"I'd rather give you a little Taser."

"Go on, go on…"

"Okay, just a taste."

"Okay. Gee, what to say? I know. Hey, remember that song of Tom's that the devil tried to tempt him with?"

"The Laughing Weasel?"

"Yeah, that's the one. Well Calvin Harris got hold of the demo tape and turned it into a dance smash. It was the big floor filler of 2015. Thomas was Number 1 for a month and gave all the money to charity."

"A lovely woman, lives in the South Bronx, still turning tricks at 87."

"Not that Charity."

"Did he ever figure out who the song was about?"

"I'd be amazed if he didn't. It really did serve remarkably well as a premonition…"

Appendix

The Laughing Weasel
(Words & music by Thomas Scrimshaw)

I am the laughing weasel
Knock me down and I'll say "Thanks for your attack"
Be kind, or just befriend me
I'll stab you in the back

I am the laughing weasel
I'm not someone you should trust, or tolerate
My smile is an illusion
My message is pure hate

(Chorus)
Weasel, Weasel
I'm on no-body's side
Beware the weasel
I'll catch you with false pride
Weasel, Weasel
Please join me for the ride
Beware the weasel
The hoarse weasel lied

I am the laughing weasel
Jean Jinnee! Yeah I practise to deceive
Just let my freak dreams sway you
Cos once caught you'll never leave

Chorus
(Middle eight, rapped)
Jingle jangle jungle jinx
Feeds you hope, the dirty minx
Gets you high on superstition
Leading lo to cataclysm
                    Repeat chorus to fade

Diabolical Liberty

Lightning Source UK Ltd.
Milton Keynes UK
UKHW02f1941200218
318208UK00011B/484/P